MAGIC RISING

MAGIC RISING

HAND OF JUSTICE™ BOOK THREE

JACE MITCHELL

MICHAEL ANDERLE

DISRUPTIVE IMAGINATION

THE MAGIC RISING TEAM

Thanks to our Beta Readers

Larry Omans
Mary Morris
Chrisa Changala
Rachel

Thanks to our JIT Readers

Angel LaVey
Micky Cocker
Larry Omans
Diane L. Smith

Editor

SkyHunter Editing Team

DEDICATION

To my best friend, Tucker.

--Jace

*To Family, Friends and
Those Who Love
to Read.
May We All Enjoy Grace
to Live the Life We Are
Called.*

— Michael

CHAPTER ONE

Willliam stared at Rendal.

The dark mage stood on a platform, a smile growing on his face. "Here is one of the spies!" he shouted into the crowd.

William was surrounded by hundreds of Sidnie's residents, all of them having come to see New Perth's "traitor."

Kris stood to Rendal's left, now grinning from ear to ear. She'd just been accused of being a spy, and moments before must have surely thought all was lost—until William threw off his cloak, screaming he was going to kick Rendal's ass.

The crowd gaped at the giant man. William removed his broadsword from his back, creating room for himself as he did. No one wanted to be in front of that weapon when he swung it.

"Rendal the Dickless!" he shouted with a devilish grin. "I think that's your new name! Let the girl go, and I won't come up there and remove whatever little manhood you have. Understand?"

The mage stepped forward, showing no concern at all for the girl. "I thought you might be the one to show up. All brawn, no brains." Rendal looked out over the crowd. "This is only *one* of the spies, but there are probably more among us right now. Don't be afraid, Sidnians. We are stronger than this one man, or a thousand like him!"

"Rendal, you couldn't lift my dick with both hands, let alone take me down. Let the damn girl go and let's stop with the shenanigans." William pushed forward, the crowd parting before him like waves before a ship. He made his way closer to the stage, his senses on high alert.

Brighten should be behind the platform now, and that was what William needed more than anything else. He hadn't told the boy *what* to do, but that was okay. Brighten wasn't an idiot and would figure it out easily enough.

"Harold," the mage called. "Come on out here, will you?"

William knew Harold just fine—the mage's fucking lackey.

Rendal's guard walked out from behind the stage, sword in his right hand.

William didn't stop pressing forward. People stared up at him with a mixture of awe and hatred on their faces. They believed the mage; he was a spy, the same as Kris up on the platform.

William stopped twenty feet from the platform. "Any of you don't want to be hurt, get outta the way now!" he commanded the crowd in front of him.

They scattered like roaches under bright light.

"Harold?" The mage spoke softly, his grin wide. "You said you can take this man, right?"

"I sure did, sir," Harold answered.

"Here's your chance." Rendal took a few steps back. "Don't kill him, though. Wound him if you must, but I want to keep him around for a little while. You know, for Riley's sake." He smirked at William.

"You're just lucky Riley ain't here, prick. She would have already handed you your balls." William looked at Harold. "And now you're sending your lackey after me? This is going to be too easy."

William's eyes blazed red and fire swooshed from his hand to his sword, lighting it.

The crowd around him moved even farther back. Even if they understood magic, they still wanted no part of this giant.

Harold stayed on the platform. Raising a hand, he waved William forward. "Come, big man. I've had enough of your mouth for a lifetime."

"I guess that's good, because I'm going to keep talkin' long after you're dead." William scanned the platform quickly, understanding the *known* dangers at least. There was Harold, of course, and Rendal would attack; William had no doubt about that.

And then there was the girl to remember. She couldn't be hurt. Kris was the reason for the whole confrontation.

Act fast, Brighten, William urged silently. He was under no illusions as to the danger ahead.

He let the fire spread up his arm, then over his sweeping shoulders, and finally down his left arm.

William ran forward, picking up speed with each step. Rendal retreated, and Harold stepped a little to the side. William knew the strategy the guard would take.

The Right Hand leapt into the air, easily clearing the platform's height.

Harold swung his sword just before William touched down, but the Right Hand's steel met it.

Flames raced up Harold's sword, trying desperately to make their way to his arm.

William thrust his shoulder forward, the flames there touching the guard as well; he shoved hard, using all his strength to send Harold flying.

Harold wasn't weak or dumb, though. He skirted to the right, flames dancing up his armor but not yet touching his vulnerable skin.

Harold brought his sword up in a weak parry, but William dashed it away. He looked at his left, extending his arm and sending a swirl of fire rolling off his fingers. The flames hit the wooden platform, spreading eagerly across the dry wood.

He just managed to bring his sword up in time to block Harold's blow.

Clang!

Harold's sword was lighter and faster and came at William again from the opposite direction. William barely got his heavier sword there in time, but he brought his forearm up after shoving it onto his own blade and pushing against Harold's.

Blood spurted from his arm, but he bore down harder.

The two stared at each other, William's fiery sword slowly moving closer to Harold's face.

William felt heat behind him, his earlier flames trying to engulf everything.

"AGHH!" William shouted, shoving with all his might.

Harold rose off the ground, unable to withstand the Right Hand's strength. He slammed the wooden platform, sliding backward.

William felt it then; the change in the air.

He ducked as a scorching ball of fire flew over his head. It slammed into the platform mere feet from him, scattering flames every which way. He turned, still crouching, and saw Rendal's bright red eyes. The crowd was fleeing, screams filling the sky.

The flames had grown swiftly, moving off the platform now to the ground.

Come on boy. Come the fuck on! William thought.

He stood as Rendal walked closer. Flames danced to the mage's left and right, and they were circling William now, too.

"Did you think you'd actually be able to use magic against *me*?" Rendal asked.

William saw the boy dashing across the stage then, the mage's back to him. He didn't let his eyes venture away from Rendal's face.

"All this power and you're still a damned moron," William retorted with a grin.

"Drop the sword and we can do this the easy way."

"I wasn't ever too good at the easy way, Rendal. I'm more of a hard way type of guy." William moved his sword into a defensive position. Sweat dripped from his brow, the heat growing more oppressive with each second.

"So be it," the mage answered.

"Hey!" Harold shouted from behind.

William wasted no time. He simply turned, flinging fire from his hands toward Harold. He knew what the guard was yelling at: Brighten and Kris hurtling across the platform.

The flames burst across Harold's chest, sending him backward again.

William whipped around toward the mage, swinging his sword where he thought the man would be.

He missed completely, spinning himself as he did.

Good, he thought, catching a glimpse of the two kids. They were off the platform and running now—fleeing for their lives.

"That wasn't smart, Right Hand," the mage chastised with a wide grin.

The smell of smoke filled William's nose and his eyes watered. If he didn't get off this pyre soon, he'd burn with it.

"You just traded yourself for two street kids." The mage shook his head in disbelief. "A strategically poor move to say the least."

"I think I'll strategically shove this fuckin' sword up your ass," William growled. He charged, ignoring the flames and smoke, hoping to create enough space for him to escape as well.

He swung, but the mage easily dodged the blade. When William brought it down in a sweeping blow, Rendal spun to the right and shoved his hand forward.

A blast of air smashed into William's back, sending him sprawling off the platform.

He slammed into the ground below chest-first, sliding across the dirt and grass.

William rolled over on his back and watched the mage

float down from the burning platform. Harold was already gone, having scampered away from the flames.

William got to a knee, then looked up at the mage. "Kill me, and let's be done with this, old man."

"Where's the fun in that?" Rendal asked.

William looked down at the dirt in front of him. He knew Riley would have been able to get out of this. She'd simply explode and burn this whole area to nothing. He couldn't do that, though.

He wasn't strong enough.

The mage was a few feet from William, flames billowing behind him.

I'll miss you, friend, he thought, meaning it.

William didn't glance up; he didn't need to. He reared his sword back and flung it with every ounce of strength he could muster.

It flew straight at the mage and William stood, bringing his hands forward. Fire blasted from his fingertips, following the soaring blade.

The mage's eyes were wide, shock on his face. He moved slightly to his right, but the blade caught his side all the same, slicing through his skin.

"AGH!" he shouted, and then the flames were on him.

A blue shield rose from the mage's body, encircling him and somehow keeping the flames from eating him alive.

William didn't give a damn what it was or how it worked. He knew this was his only chance. He had to *bolt*.

The Right Hand turned and fled, rushing across the empty expanse.

Go, Right Hand. The mage's voice filled William's head.

Rendal was laughing as he spoke. *We'll meet again. I promise. I'll tell Mason you said hello.*

Rendal watched William run away.

It was an odd sight, someone so huge fleeing someone so thin.

The flames that had hit Rendal were dying away, and for the second time in short weeks, Rendal had a flesh wound.

He looked down at himself: his right side sported a nice-sized gash and blood was leaking down his leg.

"Fuck!" he shouted.

Harold walked out from behind the flaming platform. "Do you want me to send people after him, sir?"

Rendal turned around slowly, unable to move any faster. Harold had been burnt and had a raw patch across his face. His left arm was badly singed.

"Send people after him?" the mage asked. "Who? Belarus? Maybe some of the fucking guards who serve the Prefect?"

Rendal's eyes turned red. Harold swallowed but didn't move.

"Thought you could handle him?" Rendal spat. "Thought he wouldn't be a problem for big bad Harold?"

"I hadn't expected him to have that much magic. It's grown stronger," Harold whispered.

"'Grown stronger,'" Rendal mocked. "You know what *hasn't* grown stronger? You, you fucking idiot. No. Don't go after him. He'll just kill you and everyone with you."

Rendal heard the thought in Harold's head.

"Careful," he instructed. "I'd be really careful right now if I were you, Harold."

The thought had been a simple one: *You didn't fare too well either, sir.*

And what could Rendal say? He was standing here with his side bleeding and the Right Hand having escaped.

Rendal looked at the emptied streets.

Harold walked up behind the mage. "I'm sorry, sir. I failed you."

"You'll get another chance, and Artino is working on some devices that will help," the mage told his second-in-command. "This wasn't a failure. Much of the kingdom saw what happened. If anything, an escaped spy will bind them to us stronger, which is what we want."

He looked at Harold.

"Everything serves my purpose, even this gash right here. In fact, I think it'd be a good idea to get medical attention, then I'll go see the kingdom's Royal Guard, right before the Prefect's advisors."

Rendal smiled.

"Yes, everything serves my purposes."

Brighten and Kris rushed through the kingdom's streets. They both knew where they were heading—out to the edge of Sidnie, to Shantyville.

Neither spoke. They ran in silence, Brighten completely terrified. The streets were largely empty; word had spread that the kingdom was under attack.

Spies were here, and war had just broken out in the fucking pavilion.

All of it lies, but what could Brighten do? Nothing but keep up with Kris, who was moving like greased lightning.

It took them ten minutes at full speed to reach the small shack.

Kris burst through the door. "Get packed. Right now. Whatever the fuck you have, get it packed. We've got to go."

Lucie stepped out from the back. She was cooking again; Brighten smelled it, but he couldn't care less about eating right now.

"Where's William?" Lucie asked, then, "Goodness, girl. What happened to your eye?"

"The sonsofbitches hit me," Kris responded. "It doesn't matter. We've got to get out of here right now!"

"Where's William?" Erin asked. She came out from the back as well.

"He …" Brighten choked. "He sacrificed himself so I could get to Kris."

"What do you mean, boy?" Lucie asked. "'Sacrificed himself?' Does Rendal have him?"

Brighten nodded, tears in his eyes.

"Y'all fuckin' *wish* Rendal had me," William's voice boomed from outside the ragged metal door. "He couldn't handle me on his best day, with me on my worst."

The door opened, and William practically fell through. He landed on a knee, grimacing.

Erin rushed across the shanty's dirt floor, kneeling in front of him.

"Are you okay?"

"I'm fine, my lady."

"Oh cut the 'my lady' crap!" Kris groaned. "And if you're fine, I'm a pig's titty."

Brighten's vision was still blurry, but he walked over next to Erin, barely able to believe what he was seeing. The big man was burnt in places, his flesh blackened and raw. He was dirty and looked beaten up...but he wasn't dead.

"How? How did you get away?" Brighten asked.

"Not with his brains, I can tell ya that," Kris quipped.

"Hush it, girl. You're worse than fuckin' Riley." William slowly pulled himself to his feet, favoring his side as he did.

Erin put one of his massive arms over her shoulder, doing her best to steady him.

"I don't look great, but neither does Rendal the Dickless," William bragged.

"Where's your sword?" Lucie asked.

"That's why Rendal don't look so great, I'd imagine," Verith commented.

"Besides the lady here helpin' me, Verith's the only one in this place with an ounce of fuckin' intelligence." William sat in a chair, Erin easing him down.

"I'll get water and a cloth." She hurried to the back kitchen area.

"I chucked my damned sword at the bastard," William continued. "Cut his side wide open and then tried to roast him. I think he was able to keep my flames off him, but it gave me a chance to get away."

"And now you've got no sword," Lucie chastised.

He looked up at her. "Woman, are ya mad? It was either my sword or my life. What did ya expect me to do?"

"Keep both, of course." Lucie winked at him, barely able to stifle her smile.

"Are any of you numbnuts listening to me?" Kris exclaimed. "We've got to get out of here! Now! They know where we are. That fucking...*mage* knows everything!"

"Okay, okay." Lucie walked to Kris's side and put her arm around the girl. "Let's all calm down for just a minute. I need to understand the lay of the land, and so does Verith." She looked at William. "You injured Rendal, but he'll survive?"

William nodded as Erin approached. She gave him a wet cloth and a small cup of water. "Yeah, he's gonna be okay. It just bought me some runnin' room."

"And your sword is really gone?" she asked.

"Ask again, Lucie, and I'll start using *you* as a sword," William responded.

Lucie chuckled and looked at Kris. "You're sure they know we're here?"

"One hundred percent sure," Kris answered. "I bet they're sending guards right now."

Lucie turned to Verith. "What do you want to do?"

The head general was a quiet man, and one not prone to exaggeration. He waited for a few moments, thinking about the question. "We'll need to leave here, obviously. Kids, where else is there for us to go in this city?"

"I ain't no kid," Kris shot back.

"Hush." Brighten finally spoke up. "This is serious." He looked at the general. "We could go to Connor's."

"Hell, no!" Kris shouted. "I'm not goin' nowhere near him. I don't care if that mage is standing outside and threatening to blow the whole shack down. I am *not* going to Connor."

"Who's Connor?" William asked.

"He's an *asshole*, that's who." Kris could barely contain herself.

Brighten smiled. "They have a bit of a rivalry. They both think they're the best thief on the streets."

"No. Fuck that. He *thinks* he's the best. I *know* I'm the best. I've been up to that damn tower twice now. He ain't been once." Kris was irate.

Verith ignored her, looking at Brighten. "What can Connor do for us if we go there?"

"It's a place to hide out. He'll let us stay, especially after what happened today. I imagine most of the homeless kids are scared shitless." Brighten continued, ignoring Kris's huffing and puffing.

"He'll take us five in?" Verith asked.

"Only way to find out is to go to him," Brighten answered.

"How many people live with this little twerp?" William took a sip of water.

"Who knows?" Kris was exasperated. "People fawn over him, and I can't fuckin' stand it."

"Sometimes he's by himself. Sometimes he has five or so with him. You can never tell. Kids like us aren't exactly stationary," Brighten told the group.

William stood up with a groan.

"Does this Connor have any medical supplies?" Lucie was looking at William's burns. "He's going to need some."

"He should. He's one of the only 'homeless' people I

know who doesn't move a whole lot. That's why a lot of people consider him the best." Brighten winked at Kris.

"Fuck you," she responded. "He ain't the best."

"Enough, you two twits," William grumbled. Erin had put his arm around her again, and he looked comfortable with *that* situation. "The girl twit is right. We gotta get out of here. Rendal could already be coming, and we don't have nearly enough weapons to stop him—"

"Especially not without your damned sword," Lucie quipped.

William gritted his teeth and Brighten saw him clench one of his fists.

"Calm down, big man," Kris joined in. "You might break a hip in your current condition."

"Father and Mother help me, I'm going to kill ya both before Riley ever gets here." William was trying to hold back his grin, although everyone in the room could see it.

"Okay." Verith stepped farther into the room. "She's right. We need to get out of here, and we're probably wasting too much time as it is. You two know the way to this Connor?"

"I do, but I ain't telling no one." Kris was beyond obstinate.

"I'll show ya," Brighten volunteered.

Kris stomped her foot, but there wasn't anything else she could do.

"Come on, squirt," William bellowed. "Even hurt, I can still protect ya."

"Not without that damned sword," Lucie quipped but made sure she was out of arm's reach.

CHAPTER TWO

"We've got to leave, Worth." Riley had been with The Chosen for three days now, and she couldn't take it any longer.

It wasn't being underground or training in the sweltering heat above.

It was the fact that she was away from William and the rest of the crew. That she wasn't chasing Rendal and retrieving Mason.

"No." Worth shook his head. "Not time."

"What do you mean, it's not time? I can do a hundred more things now than I could before. I'm ready, and they need my help."

"Oh?" Worth raised an eyebrow. "How you know? You Psychic?"

"I..." Riley closed her mouth. The answer to that was no. The Chosen called that type of magic "Psychic" and Riley couldn't do it at all.

Yet...

"I can tell, Worth. They're not doing well." Riley had

arrived at Worth's room a few minutes before. Eric was with them in this underground lair, but she'd left him out of this conversation.

Worth was sitting with his legs crossed, staring at the opposite wall.

He had no wine anywhere around him; it was one of the first times she'd seen him stone cold sober.

He looked at her but didn't say anything.

"Why you think something wrong?" he asked.

"I don't know. They just need me. What are *you* doing, Worth? Why are you sitting here staring at the wall?"

"Worth busy," he answered. "You need be busy. You need practice."

Riley shook her head. "No, I need to leave. *We* need to leave."

"You ask queen?" His eyebrows raised higher, and a slight grin spread over his lips.

Riley sighed and sat on the bed next to him. "No."

"Why no?"

"You know damn well why." She shook her head.

Worth laughed. "I do. Now leave me in peace. Go. Go away."

Riley couldn't tell the queen she was leaving, not alone. The woman... Well, the entire group now thought Riley was "the Chosen One."

She couldn't walk down the hallways without people showing great reverence. Literally, the two who had been massive pricks when she first arrived, Thomas and Rachel, now treated Riley with the same respect they did Queen Alexandra.

Riley *could* go tell the queen she was leaving, but the

woman would be coming too. Along with the rest of her crew.

"You still here?" Worth questioned. "I say go. You hear, right?"

He tapped the side of her head.

She slapped his hand. "Quit playing around. Tell me what you're doing in here."

He shook his head.

"Why the hell not?" Riley asked.

"It make you worry. Ask questions. *So* many questions."

"Worth, I'm going to throw you through the wall if you don't tell me what the hell you're doing. You've got no booze in here. Your lips are a human's *normal* color, which is *abnormal* for you. That means something is *not* normal."

The bald man shook his head. "Worth tell you. Not yet. Later. Now go. You give Worth headache."

She stared at him, not sure what she'd expected to get out of this encounter. She knew what she *wanted*, but Worth wasn't going to agree.

He was serious. He thought she needed more time.

As she watched, he turned his head back to the far wall and started staring again.

"Damn it, Worth. You're more frustrating than William sometimes."

Riley stood up and left the room.

Alexandra was at the other end of the hall.

"Are you serious? You followed me?" Riley asked good-naturedly. Out of everyone in these tunnels, Alexandra was the only one still treating her *somewhat* normally. Riley knew the queen still thought of her as the Chosen One, but she wasn't groveling like the rest.

"It's time to test you." The queen grinned, and Riley wasn't sure she liked the look.

"What do you mean?"

"You've been practicing these past few days, but we believe the greatest way to learn is... Well, I believe the saying is 'trial by fire.' You ready for some fire?"

Riley's eyes narrowed.

She didn't need to be asked twice. Riley fought for Justice and for New Perth, but mostly she *fought*.

"What do you have in mind?" the Right Hand asked.

"Above. Raiders are coming," the queen answered.

"How do you know?"

"Time of year. To the east, tent people are moving. They do this every year, and every year the raiders come. It's cyclical, but every year, each does it regardless of how many die."

Riley started walking down the hall. "What do the raiders want?"

"The same thing all outlaws want: Money, women, and horses."

"Will they win?" Riley asked.

"The tent people outnumber them, but they'll kill a lot, yes. They'll take a lot."

Riley looked confused. "Why do the tent people move? Why do they follow the same path every year?"

"I'd imagine it has something to do with food, but you know us now, Riley, We don't associate with non-believers. The question is, do you want to practice when the practice might mean life or death?"

"Hell yeah, I do." Riley grinned and patted the hilt of her sword.

"You smell it?" the queen asked.

Riley did—the same smell that she'd encountered before the sand wave and being brought to the Chosen.

"Yeah," she answered.

The two had traveled two hours east on camelback. Riley knew what camels were, although she'd rarely used them before. The Chosen had a handful of them that were well tended to beneath the ground, and it would have been nearly impossible for them to travel without the beasts.

Now they looked at a long caravan of people. Humans, massive folded tents, camels, other animals. It truly was majestic, and nothing she'd never seen before.

"Do *they* smell it? The burning?" Riley asked.

Alexandra nodded. "Of course they do."

"Why don't they do anything?"

The queen gestured at the expanse around her. "What would *you* do? What do you see?"

"Where are the raiders?" Riley understood what the queen meant. She saw nothing, only smelled the burning odor on the wind.

"They're moving closer, waiting for the right time. They want to strike at a weak point where there are more women than men, and preferably where there is loot as well."

Riley nodded. "But they see us, right? Why aren't they attacking us?"

"We're two women standing far from the caravan. There's no reason for them to worry. At least, that's what they *think*," the queen answered.

"So we wait?" Riley asked.

"Not too much longer, but yes."

Riley grew quiet and watched. The people of the caravan seemed to take no notice of them, yet the burning smell was constant.

"There," Alexandra whispered. "See them? The green stones?"

Riley's eyes immediately found what the queen was talking about. They were small and far in the distance but seemed to be floating in the air.

"When those start showing, the raiders are about to reveal themselves," the queen instructed.

Sure enough, Riley watched as a group of fifty people shimmered into existence. People in the caravan shrieked and started trying to run away—the women and children, at least. Men up and down the line were turning, gathering their weapons, and rushing toward the attackers.

Riley gasped. "We're too far away!" The camel she sat on wasn't going to make it across the distance in time, certainly not before the fighting started.

"You're too far away without magic, that's true." The queen dismounted her camel, landing softly in the sand.

Riley followed suit, her heart starting to beat faster in her chest.

"You can make it there in mere seconds, though, Riley." Alexandra came around her camel so that the two stood in front of the beasts, and stared at the attackers.

They were striding forward now, weapons bared. Screams rolled across the desert.

"How?" Riley was running out of hope. People were about to die.

"Your sword, of course."

Riley's eyes widened as she looked at Alexandra. "It's not going to lift me into the air and float me there!"

"When Worth gave you that sword, he told you it was magic, right? Or that it would be when you are?"

Riley nodded. "Please hurry. We're running out of time. They're going to die."

"It's magic in the sense that it will allow you to *focus* your power. You will be able to do more with it. It's an extension of you so that when you focus all your will on it, you will amplify what you can do."

Riley gritted her teeth. "How the hell is that going to get me over there? This is theory. We have *seconds* left."

"What do you need to do to get over there?" the queen asked. "Before anyone dies?"

"I'd have to fly."

The queen shrugged. "Then make it so. Pull your sword out and make it so."

Riley whipped the sword from its sheath and stared at it. She didn't have time to ask any more questions. Women and children were in trouble.

She stared at it, the green stones reflecting the sunlight.

Focus, Riley thought.

She closed her eyes, thinking of the sword.

I'd have to fly.

Then make it so.

Riley did something she would have never considered before.

Her eyes flashed open and she ran forward, her feet picking up speed and sand flying out behind her. Her focus was iron-strong, and she took her sword and thrust it into the ground while simultaneously leaping into the air.

She rose.

And rose.

And rose.

The wind whipped past her short hair, and she looked down at the caravan stretching for miles in both directions.

She was moving faster than any horse or land animal could.

She was nearly *flying*.

The descent came quickly, and screams rose into the air to meet her. Riley concentrated on her sword again.

Just before reaching the sand, she tucked and rolled. She brought herself to a stop quickly, whipping around so that she faced the coming raiders.

Their animals squealed as the raiders brought them to a halt.

"Where are you kiddos going?" Riley asked, flashing a grin, her eyes still blazing red.

"What the fuck is *she?*" the raider in front shouted.

"*WHERE DID SHE COME FROM?*" someone else yelled.

The caravan was quiet behind her, and Riley could tell they were paying attention. Wondering if she were friend or foe.

"Oh, I just floated down from the heavens," Riley quipped. "Probably best you all just head the opposite way. Try again next year. Whaddaya say?"

"Fuck this," someone called from behind. The group of fifty were all here now. "I don't care if she's got magic.

We've got the numbers. Take her, and then we'll get the rest."

"I was hoping you'd say that." Riley caught a quick glimpse around the crowd of Alexandra in the distance. The queen hadn't moved. She was leaving this completely in Riley's hands.

Which was fine with her.

The raiders jumped off their mounts, brandishing swords and knives.

Riley closed her eyes momentarily. She'd practiced a lot so far, but nothing like this. Not with so *many*.

William's gonna piss his pants when he sees everything I can do, she thought.

Riley opened her eyes as someone swung a sword at her neck.

She ducked, her own sword striking out like a serpent and cutting the man through the gut.

She straightened as he fell to the side, screaming. "Come on, you got to be tougher than *that*. I want to use some *magic*."

They came then, all at once. Riley should have died—no doubt about it.

But she didn't.

Instead, she shoved her sword into the ground and jumped again, this time rising straight up and twirling as she did.

The sand around the attackers started swirling, increasing in speed as she rose.

She looked down at the raiders, the sand beating at them. Hitting them so hard that their skin was beginning to bleed.

Their screams met her ears, and she smiled. They'd been planning to rape and kill. They were getting what they deserved.

Riley dropped her sword point-first. She didn't look at it as she fell, but rather *felt* it.

She turned her palm downward and fire rushed out, catching up with the falling weapon.

The sword drove into the sand hilt-deep, and the flames hit directly after. They spread as if oil had been spread across the ground, creating an inferno beneath the raiders' feet.

Riley started her descent as the people below rolled on the ground in agony.

When her feet touched down, the fire died beneath them. She looked across the intervening space to the caravan.

It was no longer moving. Everyone stared at her.

"You'll be safe for today," she told them.

"What are you?" one of the caravan women asked. "I've never seen anything like you in my whole life."

Riley's eyes faded to their usual color. She didn't know how to answer the question. She was no different now than she'd been six months ago.

"I'm the Right Hand of New Perth."

The woman nodded. "Thank you."

Riley smiled bashfully. "It's... Well, it's my job, I guess."

"Come on, Bashful Betty!" the queen called. "Let's go!"

Riley shook her head and reached for her sword. She lifted it from the sand easily, the metal clean and smooth as always.

"Thank you again," the woman whispered. "You saved our lives."

Riley nodded. She wished she could say that she would do more, but she couldn't. She was going to find Mason; that was where her duty lay.

"No." Worth shook his head. "It not time."

They were back under the ground, and this time the three sat in Alexandra's quarters.

"I agree with him, Riley," the queen told her.

Riley had brought up her earlier demand to both Worth and Alexandra. She needed to leave.

"I came here to learn how to release my magic. I can now. What other purpose do I have here?" She was growing irate with Worth, more so than with Alexandra. Worth was resolute in his refusal to leave. He wasn't even drinking down here. He was out of wine.

Yet he said she wasn't ready.

"Rendal still too strong," Worth told her, although he only looked at the queen. "You lose, you try now. Need more training."

"You can't keep me here." Riley felt like she might explode. She looked at Alexandra. "Neither of you can, and you both know it."

"I know, Riley," the queen agreed. "None of the Chosen would try to make you stay against your will. This mage you're talking about, though. Worth says he's strong—"

"Aye, strong," Worth interrupted.

"Worth isn't any slouch with his own magic, yet he's

saying this Rendal is too powerful to attack right now. If he's saying it, I trust him. What you did out there with the raiders was nothing."

She leaned forward.

"I mean that, Riley. It was *nothing*. If you reach your potential, you will eclipse anyone on this continent."

"It'll be enough. They need me," Riley responded.

"They fine," Worth told her.

"How do *you* know?" Riley felt like she might snap.

"I see them. Worth look. They... They okay."

Riley turned all the way in her chair so that she was facing Worth. "What do you mean, you *see* them?"

"Psychic magic. Worth do. Not good, but little. Worth see them."

Riley stood. "And you didn't tell me?"

"You need practice. Worth watch. You worry. Everything fine."

Riley couldn't remember the last time she'd been so angry with anyone, let alone Worth.

"What did you see?"

"They fine. You practice. Worth make sure they fine," he answered, but he still wouldn't look at her.

Riley turned to the queen. "Can you see them?"

"No. Not without having met them. Psychic magic isn't my strong suit, either."

"Are they hurt, Worth?" Riley turned back to the tent leader.

"Not bad."

"Not *badly*? That ends it. I'm leaving. I'm going now." Riley turned to the door and started walking across the room.

Worth stood and faced her. "*You*. Not. Ready."

Riley put one hand on the door handle. "I have to help them."

"You no help. You get hurt. They get *more* hurt. This what he wants. This his whole plan."

Riley knew the arguments, and she didn't care anymore. If William or Lucie or Mason—or anyone else—was hurt, she had to help. She had to get there instead of remaining holed up under the ground.

"I'm going, Worth. I'm taking Eric with me, back to his mother." Without turning around, she said, "Alexandra, can one of you show me how to get to Sidnie? Can you spare someone to take me?"

"I'm torn here, Riley."

"Well, be torn with Worth. I'm not. I know what I have to do. Can you spare someone?"

The queen chuckled. "Riley, we are yours to command. I may be their queen, but you are our Chosen One. We can all go, or we can all stay. It is up to you to decide. If you go, we will be able to help you find lodging in Sidnie. We still have connections there."

Riley sighed and looked down at her feet. She didn't want that mantle, but at the same time, she couldn't shake it. They wouldn't let her; it didn't matter what she said.

"Fine. I'll take Thomas. I'll send him back once I'm there. I'll make sure no harm comes to him."

"Whatever you wish, Riley. I'm not worried about your safety, not like Worth. You may be making a mistake," the queen said, "but your safety is guaranteed. You will prevail; it may just take longer than you want. You are the Chosen One."

Riley ignored her. "Worth, are you coming or staying?"

"Need wine. You too stubborn. Worth come, but need be drunk deal with you."

With her back to the bald man, Riley grinned. "Alexandra, is there anything down here he can drink?"

"I'm sorry, but no. We don't partake," the queen answered.

Worth sighed. "This be longest trip of Worth's life."

Riley couldn't help but laugh.

CHAPTER THREE

"What the hell are we gonna do?" William blurted.

"If I remember correctly," Lucie interjected, "weren't you telling us all two days ago that everyone should listen to you about everything? Now you're asking *us* what to do?"

William brought his hands to his head and groaned. "I never thought I'd say this, but I want Riley back. I want her here so we can kill you and the little sass mouth who's now your sidekick."

"It'd take the two of you," Kris laughed. "'Cause you alone can't do much, fatso."

"He's right." Brighten tried refocusing the discussion. "We need to figure out what comes next."

Brighten had been quiet for much of the day. That was his go-to, especially with this group of loudmouths.

They'd gotten to Connor's last night. Brighten had left to head back to his magic class, but the rest remained inside. Even Kris hadn't ventured out.

From what Brighten heard, she hadn't liked that one bit.

Brighten didn't have that big a problem with Connor. He was older, and honestly, Brighten thought Kris might just have a crush on him.

In any case, Connor had let them in graciously enough and was staying out of their way. He hadn't asked any questions. Connor was smart. He knew what was going on —to a degree, at least—and if he was harboring fugitives or spies, well... He'd die the moment he was caught.

No questions asked.

Connor wasn't going to tell anyone.

"You learn anything last night in school, kid?" William asked.

Brighten nodded. "Yeah, some. This mage is good, no doubt about it, but everything is so *aggressive.*"

"What do you mean?" Lucie questioned.

"Thought you were supposed to be some kind of master mage?" William grinned. "Aggressive, Lucie, means to *attack.*" He winked at Brighten before looking back at Lucie. "Stick with me, gal. I'll teach you some things."

"Only thing you can teach anyone is how to shake your dick when you're done pissin', and probably not well," Lucie retorted. She focused back on Brighten. "He's teaching you to use magic *against* others? Is that what you mean?"

Brighten nodded. "Yeah. He's calling us warrior mages."

"Brighten," Lucie continued, "How are you handling the class? Rendal... He can tell almost anything about anyone. And Kris here explained you have a predilection for magic, but you're not exactly up to par with everyone else there, right?"

"Yeah," Brighten answered. "I mean, I'm behind, but I'm catching up fast. Rendal hasn't shown any interest in me at all, which is good. Don't mean I'm not scared, though."

"He's scared of his own shadow," Kris remarked with a grin.

"Yeah, well, I'm not the one hiding out in here all day and night. Hard to get scared when ya ain't doin' nothin'." Brighten turned his head to Connor's room. "I wonder if Connor just sits around all day doin' nothin'? You think that's how he got to be the best?"

"Careful, twerp, or I'll break your hands," Kris snapped. "Hard to steal anything when your fingers don't work."

"Oh, you two pipsqueaks hush. Neither of ya would bust a grape in a food fight." William stood up. "Back to my original question, since I'm the only one with any brains around here. What the hell are we going to do? I can't very well go out there and fix anything, given what happened."

He looked at Verith.

"Any ideas, general?"

Verith nodded. "I've been thinking. The reason we're here is simple: to observe and understand what Rendal's plan is while Riley learns her powers. So far..." He shrugged. "We haven't done too well at that endeavor, at least the observing part."

"Wonder whose doin' that was?" Lucie grinned.

"Sorry, old lady," William shot back. "Had to save some kiddos while you were at the shack stirrin' stew."

"We've become active players," Verith continued as if

not hearing the two. "But Rendal doesn't care about us, does he, Lucie?"

"Not for more than to hurt Riley."

Verith nodded. "So what do we know? He's building a warrior-mage class. He's planted the rumor in the citizenry that New Perth is actively spying on them. They've got to be gearing up for war in other ways, too. The military must be readying itself."

"All right." William was pacing now.

Erin stood against the wall watching him. Brighten noticed the two seemed to always be in close proximity to each other.

"But still," the big man asked, "what the hell do we do?"

"Well, fatso and I are out," Kris commented. "We can't show our faces anywhere. I'm shocked damned Brighten here can still be seen in the streets after grabbing me off the platform."

"It's 'cause I stole the show, pipsqueak. Like I always do."

"More like stole all the damned food in the castle," Kris quipped. "I swear you gain five pounds a day now."

Erin finally spoke up. "That leaves me, Verith, and Brighten."

William's eyes widened. He stopped pacing and stared at her.

"Oh, goodness, here we go. The chivalrous knight." Kris rolled her eyes.

William said nothing, although he blushed slightly.

"Seriously, if we're thinking rationally, it's us three. The rest of you are compromised." She looked at William and shrugged. "So if we have that constraining us, how do we make it work?"

The room fell quiet for a few moments.

"We need to get inside the military," Verith mused. "We need to understand what's happening there."

"And how do we do that?" William grumbled.

"Kris, you just gonna act like you got nothin' to say?" It was Connor, speaking loudly through the thin door to his bedroom.

All eyes went to Kris.

"Shut the fuck up, Connor!" She shook her head multiple times hard. "Not happening. I'm serious. Not. Happening."

"What's he talkin' about, pipsqueak?" William asked.

"He's making up shit, that's what." Kris was still shaking her head.

William looked at Brighten. "Who's makin' up what, kid?"

Brighten winced. He knew Kris's righteous fire was about to be tossed on him. "Ehhh, Connor might not be making up *everything*." His voice was a high squeak, like a rusty door closing.

"Shut up, Brighten! Or I'm gonna shut you up!"

Brighten closed one eye, unable to look at the world fully. He wanted to just crawl into a hole and die.

"It's okay, kid. She ain't gonna hurt nothin'. Tell me what this Connor boy is talkin' about." William moved closer to Brighten, putting himself between the kid and Kris.

"Connor! Tell 'em!" Brighten shouted, still looking at

his feet. He didn't want to say another damned word about it.

"Ha!" Connor shouted from his room. "You're the one who made her your best friend. Not me. You go ahead and take that bitch's wrath. I ain't!"

Brighten groaned.

"Enough!" William growled. "I'm gonna start bashing brains in if I don't get some answers. What does the pipsqueak know about the military?"

Brighten went ahead and closed both eyes, knowing that death was coming. He simply accepted it. "Her brother is a guard for the castle. That's how we get in."

"Damn right it is!" Connor shouted. "That's why it don't count that you made it to the fuckin' top. Cheaters, the lot of ya!"

"I'm not doing it," Kris whispered. "I'm not involving him in this anymore."

Erin moved across the room, putting her hand on Kris's arm. Kris tried to pull away, but Erin didn't let her. "I know what you're going through. How hard this must be for you."

Kris looked at her. "How the hell could you know?"

Erin smiled, a sad thing. "I have a son. He's not here because I've involved him in a different area of this. You saw that mage up close, didn't you?"

Kris turned her eyes to the floor. She nodded.

"You know how dangerous he is?" Erin asked.

Kris nodded again.

"We all have to give something. The people in this room, William, Lucie, and Verith...They've all been willing to give their lives," Erin told her.

"It's not *my* life," Kris disputed. "It's my *brother's* life."

"He loves Sidnie? This kingdom?"

Kris nodded, and Brighten knew she was telling the truth. Her brother Billy owed everything to Sidnie, including the very fact that he was off the streets and making something of himself. In another kingdom, that might not have been possible.

"Then the choice isn't yours to make, darlin'." Erin's smile was warm, and she put an arm around Kris's shoulder. "It's your brother's because he's got to know something is really, really wrong here."

Kris's eyes shot to Brighten. He wanted to flee. "You're a dick."

"Nah, pipsqueak, he's just finally letting his dick hang a little bit," William interrupted with a wide grin. "Getting brave, ain'tcha, kid?"

Brighten didn't feel brave. He felt like Kris might rip his eyeballs right from their sockets.

Verith interjected. "The next question is, who do we send?"

"Oh, that's easy," Erin said. "Me."

William whipped around, his laughter forgotten. "No! No way! You're not going anywhere near that psycho!"

Kris started chuckling. "Oh, no, fatso. You don't get to let her lecture me about everyone needing to do their part, then turn around and say she can't do hers."

"Now listen here!" William yelled, pointing his finger right at Kris. He looked like he had something else to say. At least for a moment, but then his face grew confused.

"Cat got your tongue?" Lucie asked.

"You… You… Just hush! She's not goin', and that's final!" William shouted, still pointing his finger.

Erin moved across the room toward the Right Hand. "William, I know you're concerned, but I'm a big girl. Remember, I sailed the seas for years before you found me. I can take care of myself."

William's face relaxed some, but not because she was convincing him. It was clear he'd thought of something.

"You can't do it. You're a woman. They're not going to let some strange *woman* join the military."

Kris smiled and looked straight at William. "You're not from around here, are ya?"

"Watch it, pipsqueak."

"Our military works on quotas, fatso," Kris continued. "Fifty percent women, fifty percent men. Our last Prefect was a woman. We like to keep things fair here, so Erin will fit right in with the military."

William's face dropped. "She doesn't need to go. Verith should go instead."

"They're more likely to tell I'm not from here. My training is too ingrained. They won't think I'm just some person off the street."

"Yeah," Kris volunteered. "He walks and talks like someone shoved a stick up his ass. Ain't nobody buyin' that this guy ain't with some sort of military through and through. Most likely, they'll just think he's a spy. Erin's the only one."

"So it's settled. I'll go, find out what's happening, and report back." Erin grinned, and as William started to say something, she leaned in and gave him a kiss on the cheek.

His face turned bright red.

"Uh, uh, uh…"

"I'll give it to you, fatso," Kris quipped. "You're much better with a sword than you are women."

"This the one?" Billy asked.

"She's the one," Kris answered. Kris didn't like this, not one bit, but Erin had been right. They all had a part to play here, every citizen of Sidnie, because their kingdom was being usurped and almost no one knew it.

Billy hadn't been a dick, either. He understood, perhaps even better than Kris. When she'd told him their plan, his only response had been, "I'll help any way I can. What's going on inside this castle? It's beyond frightening."

"I'm wonderin' if she's too pretty," Billy observed.

Erin remained silent, clearly letting the siblings work this out.

"You ain't no damned sexist, Billy, so shut it with all that," Kris told him.

"You can be dumb as rocks sometimes," her brother said without looking at her. His eyes remained on Erin, narrow and clinical. "It's got nothin' to do with bein' sexist. Pretty women like this don't usually sign up for the military. Pretty women like this usually marry rich and never look at the people serving in the military. All I'm saying is, she might be suspect."

"I can fit in," Erin promised. "That won't be a problem."

Billy shrugged. "Right now, it might not even matter. The military leaders couldn't find their asses with both hands. There's so much confusion going on, she can probably just slip in. I'll make sure she's wearing the right garb."

"Why's there so much confusion?" Erin asked.

"Well, that magic school for one. It's so new, the entire bureaucracy is having to change to make room for it. The kingdom used to leave that up to the citizenry, ya know?"

Erin nodded. "So now the military doesn't have the necessary focus on it?"

"Exactly," Billy agreed. "Hell, I could probably skip my shift tonight and nobody would notice."

"He acts like he's so important," Kris chimed in. "They probably haven't noticed him in six months."

She grinned at her brother.

"Keep talkin' and I'll arrest ya," Billy shot back. He looked at Erin again. "Yeah, I'm with you. Let's get you in the military and find out what we can. I'd do it myself, but they'd notice that. I can't run duty as a guard and as a foot soldier. That won't work."

"When do we get started?" Erin asked.

"They're running the military around the clock," Billy explained. "Three shifts. It's a fuckin' mess, but the orders are to get everyone ready for war, and anyone who can use magic is being pulled out and put in the damn school. It's creating more confusion. We'll get you in on the night shift. That's when they're running the top class for the magic school, so there will be fewer people with eyes on the army, get it?"

Erin nodded and smiled. "I get it."

"You here for the double-time pay?"

The whisper came from Erin's side. She was standing at attention, listening to someone barking orders from far ahead of her.

"Here to stop the damned spies," Erin whispered back without looking over.

"Ha! If you believe that, I've got some oceanfront property to sell you in the Badlands."

Erin did her best to hold back a grin. "What do you mean?"

"I mean," the woman next to her said, "I'm here because they're payin' double-time. No other reason."

"You don't believe New Perth is trying to attack us?" Erin didn't like talking, especially right now, but she wanted to know what the citizens were thinking.

"Why would they attack us? Don't make no damn sense, and anyone with two brain cells can see that. But I ain't too concerned. They want to pay me double-time for joinin' the army, I'm in."

"How long have you been here?" Erin whispered.

"Third night. Gettin' used to sleepin' days now, and they pay at the end of each shift. Make sure they don't cheat ya, girlie. Cheap bastards."

A soldier was walking down Erin's line, so both women quit talking.

The man stopped in front of Erin.

"You're new."

You're smart, Erin wanted to say. Instead, "Yes, sir. Here to help the cause."

"And what cause is that?" the soldier asked. He looked like he didn't trust her right off the bat.

Billy had been right. A lot of the other women within the ranks weren't the prettiest, but it could just be the soldier was actively looking for spies.

"Making sure New Perth doesn't wipe us off the map," Erin answered. "I was at the square the other day, sir. I saw what they're capable of."

The soldier nodded. "I'm glad you did. The threat is real."

He stared at her for another second, seeming to take her measure.

"Glad you joined. We need every able-bodied person we can find."

"Yes, sir," Erin responded.

The soldier walked off.

The woman next to her made a loud farting noise with her mouth.

Erin couldn't help but smile then.

"These damned soldiers are all brainwashed or dumb. I don't know which," the woman said. "But I don't care, either. I'll take this double-time pay until the war starts, then I don't know what I'm gonna do."

"*INTO GROUPS!*" the commanding officer shouted from the front.

"Time to get movin'," the woman said. "Good luck."

Erin caught a glimpse of her as she walked to the right. She was short, stocky, and looked strong.

"Newbies with me!" a woman to the left shouted.

Erin definitely understood what Billy meant about the place being unorganized. She nearly shook her head as she hustled across the large room to the shouting woman.

She fell into line and listened.

Minutes passed as the woman droned on about the need to stop spies, just more bullshit that Erin tuned out. She knew why she was here, and *this* was not it.

When she finished talking, they started running basic drills. It was all easy for Erin; things she'd taught her son years ago.

They paired up for some light hand-to-hand combat. The commander didn't care whether the sexes mixed, so Erin found herself in front of a strong-looking man.

"You're way too hot to be in here." He winked at her.

Erin ignored him and looked at the sergeant standing next to their mat. "We ready?"

"Don't look at *her*, missy," the man interjected with mock sweetness. "I'm the one that's about to put you down. If you want, I can lay you down in a more comfortable place after."

Erin turned her head and stared at the man, her usual warm smile nowhere to be seen.

He wasn't ugly, but *rough*. It was clear he'd grown up poor, but that wasn't any excuse for poor manners.

"How're your balls feeling?" Erin asked, finally flashing a smile.

The man looked a bit stunned by the question but smiled back, thinking he was getting somewhere with her. "They're good now, but I bet you can make 'em feel a lot better."

Still smiling, Erin quipped, "By the end of this, you're not gonna be able to sit down for a week because they're gonna hurt too bad."

The man's smile dropped and he sneered, clearly not taking the rebuke well.

Erin only smiled wider.

"All right, you two newbs done?" the sergeant asked. "Go ahead and get started."

"Gladly," Erin responded.

The man crouched, looking like he had some idea of what he was doing.

He'd been in bar fights, but probably no more.

Erin loosened up, letting her arms dangle at her sides before bringing her hands up in fists in front of her.

"Come and get it," the man growled, taking a more defensive posture.

Erin smiled. "Fine by me."

She moved forward gracefully. She'd never have her son's prowess—or Riley's—but Erin knew what she was doing in hand-to-hand combat.

She feigned a jab. The man moved slightly out of the way and quickly tried to counter, sending a hard punch at Erin's jaw.

Erin ducked, then rapidly stood up and let fly a ruthless roundhouse.

The man never knew what hit him.

She connected with the back of his jaw and saw his eyes glaze, out cold on his feet.

He remained like that for a second, maybe two, then collapsed to the ground.

Erin opened and closed her fist a few times, then turned to the sergeant. "What else ya got?"

"Captain!" the sergeant called. "I think we need to get this one out of the newbs!"

Erin smiled. Taking over an entire military might be fun.

Brighten saw Erin walking back to Connor's, but he didn't get close. It was late at night for both of them, or early in the morning, depending on how you looked at it. Brighten was tired, but Erin appeared to still have some energy.

He didn't know if she saw him; he remained in the shadows as he walked, keeping his distance. He turned down different alleys and pathways, doing his best to make any prying eyes think the two didn't know each other.

Finally, they reached Connor's place. Brighten was actually impressed with the boy. While he and Kris had had to bounce around from spot to spot, Connor had managed to hold onto this little shack for a good bit of time.

He might actually be able to go straight; quit the life of theft and pickpocketing.

Brighten waited outside for a few minutes after Erin went in, checking to make sure they hadn't been followed. Once he thought they were safe, he slipped in the back door.

Connor's place wasn't any mansion. He had a bedroom, and there was a large main room. William's crew stayed in the larger space, and Kris was forced to as well. Brighten was able to come and go as he pleased.

"How was class?" Lucie asked as he walked in.

"Draining."

Brighten went to a corner and sat.

Everyone in the room was up, despite the late hour. They were starting to get a routine going. Brighten would come home and tell them what he'd learned, and they'd ask questions and then strategize.

Now Erin had information to give as well, and Brighten was glad for it.

He was *exhausted*.

"Thanks for showin' up, kid," William quipped. "You see how fast she got here, don't you?"

He gestured to Erin.

Brighten didn't have the energy to retort.

"Oh, hush, William," Erin shot back. "Brighten was behind me the whole way. He kept his distance so that people wouldn't suspect anything."

"You pay her to cover for you?" William asked with a wink.

"All of ya, can we focus?" Lucie interjected. "We need to know what's goin' on with the military."

"No discipline," Kris said. "The lot of ya. As wild as toddlers."

William rolled his eyes, then glanced at Erin. "My lady, I apologize. Please tell us what happened."

Kris looked like she wanted to say something, but a sharp elbow from Lucie kept her mouth shut.

"Well, most of the people they're recruiting aren't worth a damn. From what I can gather, not *everyone* believes what the mage is saying."

"Whatcha mean?" Kris asked.

"Well, I talked to at least three people during the evening who told me they flat out didn't think there were any spies. They thought this was some kind of weird change of power, or they weren't thinking about it at all. They were more concerned about getting paid."

Kris smiled at that, and Brighten did too. Neither

wanted to think of their kingdom as a bunch of easily fooled idiots.

"What did you see?" Lucie asked.

"A lot. I mean, they're preparing for war without any doubt. If the citizens aren't buying the official line en masse, the upper brass of the military is." Erin walked across the room and grabbed a small tin of water.

She took a sip and continued.

"I wouldn't be concerned with the troops that much, at least not those I've seen."

"They also just started," Verith commented. "They'll grow deadlier, the more they train."

"True," Erin agreed. "I'm more concerned about the rumors I heard."

Brighten had closed his eyes, listening but trying to rest as well. He opened them at the mention of rumors.

"Go on," Lucie prodded.

Erin smiled. "But it's fun making you all wait. Especially him." She walked over and poked William in the back.

"I'm gonna vomit." Kris touched her stomach and bent over mockingly, "if you two don't quit flirtin'."

"Jealous, pipsqueak?" William called, although his face was red.

Erin turned to Lucie. "People are talking about weapons. Not swords or bows and arrows. They're talking about magical weapons."

"Say that again," Verith commanded.

Erin looked at him. "Magical weapons."

"People talk," William grumbled. "The dumber the person, the more they talk—"

"Which is why *you* never shut up," Kris got in.

William ignored it. "So if you got a bunch of dumb people in that military, they're going to be talking a hell of a lot."

"I'd agree if it was only the citizens talking," Erin responded. "But I saw other things, too. The captains and sergeants—they're very careful to keep everyone out of certain areas."

"What areas?" Verith asked.

"Well, we train in two main places. One is the castle's back lawn, and the other is the castle's gymnasium. I'm sure there are other places, but for this new crew, that's where we're at."

Erin squatted. The shack's floor was dirt, of course, and she drew a box.

"This is one part of the gymnasium. The part we're allowed in. Here, on the left..." She drew another box. "We're allowed in there, too. But to the right..." She drew a third box. "No one goes in there."

Verith's brow creased. "The gymnasium. You think they're hiding weapons in the *gymnasium*? That seems like a poor place to hide anything, especially if you're training next to it."

"True." Erin nodded. "All I know is that they won't let anyone in there. The other side is fine, but if anyone so much as looks at the right side of the gym, they get an earful."

Lucie looked at Verith. "I agree with you. It doesn't make any sense that they would hide weapons in such a place. I mean, surely the kingdom has to have better places to put things. *Important* things."

"Well, let's say you're right, and it's not weapons in there," Erin commented. "*Something* is in there. Or, at least, there's a reason they won't let anyone near it."

Brighten closed his eyes again. He didn't know who was going to volunteer the information, him or Kris. He wanted *her* to. He had enough going on with this damned magic class.

"Why's she lookin' at you, kid?" William's voice cracked across the room.

Brighten still didn't open his eyes. He knew why Kris was looking at him—the same reason he *wasn't* looking at her.

"One of you gonna speak up, or am I gonna have to bash your heads together?" William asked.

"Brighten?" Kris said.

He only shook his head. "I don't know what any of you are talkin' 'bout."

"He's such a fuckin' wimp," Kris spat. "Gets my brother dragged into this and then just sits in the corner and won't say another word."

Brighten opened only one eye to see if Kris was actually pissed.

No, she had that shit-eating grin on her face.

"The two of ya are about ten seconds away from only eatin' soft foods for the rest of yer lives." William stood up.

Neither Brighten nor Kris thought he was actually threatening, only blustering.

Brighten finally groaned. "You don't know how fuckin' tiring this is, Kris!"

"Oh, boo hoo. I'm stuck in here with this smelly ogre all day and night while you get to wander around freely."

"Will one of you please tell us what's going on?" Verith asked.

"He's such a baby." Kris turned to the others. "Of *course* there are places that the kingdom hides things. They've been doing it for years. *We* know where they are."

"You and Brighten?" William asked.

"Who else would I be talkin' about, numbskull?" Kris grinned.

"Where would they hide weapons if not in the gymnasium?" Lucie asked.

"Beneath the castle," Kris said. "There are crypts down there that probably stretch for miles. I don't know since I've only seen the entrance, but they exist, and that's where they're going to hide anything valuable."

"Can you take us to them?" William asked.

Kris laughed. "You get dumber by the day, big man. There's no *us*. You and I ain't going nowhere, especially not toward the castle." Kris looked at Erin and Brighten. "Them two can, though. They've got pretty much free rein in the place right now."

Brighten groaned again, opening his other eye. "When do you want me to do it, Kris? When I'm resting from class or in class? When do you think would be a good time to slink around the castle and look for secret weapons?"

Kris shrugged, grinning slyly. "I don't know. I managed to find the time to involve my brother in this, so I figure you can find the time to go look through some tunnels."

William looked at Erin. "What are you thinking, my lady?"

"She's thinkin' you need to quit sounding so lame." Kris was having a grand time.

"I think we have to go and see," Erin answered, then looked at Brighten.

"If you show me where the crypts are, I can check by myself. You don't have to go down there with me."

Brighten sighed. He was looking at Kris, seeing the light in her eyes. She was ready to jump all over him the moment he said he'd be fine with showing Erin so long as he didn't have to go into them.

Another groan.

"I'm not gonna listen to her mouth for days on end because I sent you down there alone. We'll go tomorrow night when we're both done with our... Fuck, our *jobs*, I guess."

Everyone in the room chuckled.

"The kid is growin' up." William walked over and tousled Brighten's hair. He looked at Kris. "If he keeps training with magic, you're gonna need to watch out, pipsqueak."

"Please. If he's anything like you, I don't have to worry 'bout nothin'." She looked at Lucie. "I mean, this joker lost his sword, didn't he?"

"Aye." Lucie grinned wide. "Still ain't got no sword, William."

Brighten looked up at the big man. He was grinning broadly.

"Wait 'til I get another sword and he gets a little magic. Both of you brats are gonna rue the day you spoke so carelessly. Tell 'em, kid."

Brighten groaned, closing his eyes. "I don't wanna go down there!"

William sighed and shook his head. "Gonna be tough to

have an 'us versus them' mentality with a sob story like this one."

Kris winked at William. "Told you. You're both softer than baby shit!"

William looked down at him. "You got to toughen up, kid. If you don't, Riley's gonna run right over you when you meet her."

The Royal Guard stood before Rendal—five knights, all of them mages. Rendal had asked the Prefect about his Guard, coming to understand that they were more or less Sidnie's Right Hands. Each had a command beneath them.

These five were the strongest.

For Rendal to prevail here, he had to vanquish these wannabe heroes first, then turn his attention to the Prefect's advisors.

"Where is the Prefect?" the knight in the middle asked.

Rendal had sent word through Slidell that the leader wanted to see his Royal Guard. Now they all stood outside at one of the Guards' training rooms, the Prefect having said he wished to see them in action.

"He couldn't make it," Rendal answered.

"And you are?"

"I'm... I guess you could say I'm the new boss around here." Rendal smiled.

The knights looked at each other, their swords rattling slightly with their bodies' movement.

The middle Guard turned back to Rendal. "You're that

merchant everyone's been talking about. Where's the Prefect?"

"He is..." Rendal shrugged. "I've misplaced him, but I'm here in his stead."

The middle knight unsheathed his sword first, the other four immediately following suit.

The outdoor area was far from the prying eyes of anyone else. The Guard liked to practice in private. They now occupied a space with thick wooden logs standing upright which was used for sword practice. Other weapons of war were scattered throughout the area. Quivers with arrows sat in front of targets. A covered pavilion with three walls contained axes, swords, and shields.

Rendal began pacing back and forth in front of the knights.

"I thought about what to do with you five, you know? I gave it serious consideration." He nodded, looking down at his feet as he walked. "I could use a group of men like you on my side, truth be told. Yet...the advisors are more important. I can get strength anywhere, but I need the leaders on board."

Rendal stopped and turned around, heading back the other way. He could sense the knights' apprehension growing, yet they'd heard about this merchant's importance. They weren't going to simply attack him.

At least not yet.

"So," Rendal continued. "What do I do? Convince you all to join my cause or eliminate you?"

"This man is mad," one of the knights said. "We need to find the Prefect."

Rendal paid them no mind. "If I eliminate you I can use

your death to turn the advisors, which is more important. Plus, none of you have Riley's power. You might know magic, but your potential is simply..."

Rendal stopped and looked at the five knights.

"Your potential is lacking."

His eyes flashed bright red as a devilish grin spread over his face.

"Do you wish to attack the Royal Guard, merchant?" the middle knight asked. The other four were spreading out, their own eyes turning red.

"No, of course not," Rendal answered. "I wish to *kill* the Royal Guard."

The arrows across the field sprang from their quivers and flew across the field toward the five knights.

The one on the right turned to face them, his left hand rising as he tried to force them back.

The other four moved forward, swords raised.

"Four against one seems a bit unfair." Rendal raised his right hand, and the weapons beneath the pavilion pulled themselves from the walls on which they hung.

The weapons also raced across the distance.

The knights saw the danger now. They weren't fighting a single man, but multitudes.

The knight facing the arrows couldn't force them down. He flung flames at them, but it was too late. They were too close to burn away completely.

They flew through the flames, impaling the knight.

He let out a sharp groan as his body tensed, five arrows piercing his body.

He fell to the ground.

The knight on Rendal's left launched himself forward. He slashed with his sword, but Rendal stepped back lithely.

The weapons were fifty feet away now, rushing at the remaining three guards who had turned to try to battle them.

Electricity ripped from Rendal's left hand, bright strands of light that reached for the attacking knight's sword. They grabbed the metal blade, rapidly tracing down it to the knight's gloved hand.

The knight started shaking, unable to let go of the sword as the electricity gripped him.

Rendal grinned while he electrocuted the man.

The group of flying weapons slammed into the three knights still living.

No, they were definitely not as strong as Riley. They couldn't face both Rendal and the fifteen or so swords, axes, and shields about to batter them.

They swung their own swords, ducking and dodging, fighting weapons whose owner controlled them with magic instead of his hands.

Rendal moved behind the fighting knights.

He wouldn't make them suffer. He didn't have time. He had to meet with the advisors momentarily.

Rendal lifted his right hand into the air and touched three separate places with his index finger, fireballs sprouting each time.

The fireballs grew in size, spinning in front of Rendal. His eyes were alight as the blades and axes slashed at the knights.

Riley wouldn't have behaved like them. She would have focused only on eliminating the real threat: Rendal. Plus, her magic was much more powerful than these feeble heroes.

The fireballs shot forward.

Each struck its target, exploding across the designated knight. Fire raced over their bodies and screaming filled the air.

Then Rendal's axes and swords hit home too.

The Royal Guard, the Prefect's protectors, lay on the ground, the strongest now eliminated.

The red in Rendal's eyes faded.

Easy enough. Now to go let the advisors know what would be asked of *them*.

The advisors sat around a circular wooden table. There were ten of them, and they took up most of the table. Normally there would have been only one open chair, but now two remained.

They were for the Prefect and Rendal.

Lawrence Slidell walked into the room first, Rendal following.

Harold came last, taking a place against the wall.

The Prefect had called the meeting after the advisors had grown more and more concerned. At least, it *appeared* that the Prefect had called the meeting. In reality, Rendal pulled the strings.

"Hello," the Prefect said as he took his seat.

Rendal waited, standing behind and to the left of Slidell.

This had been planned, of course.

"Hello, Prefect Slidell," the group said almost as one.

A man on the right spoke up. Rendal knew his name, just as he knew everyone's name in the room. This one was Terry.

"We were hoping this would be an audience with just you, Prefect."

"I...know," Slidell stammered. The man was little more than a shell at this point. "You...all need to...meet Rendal Hemmons."

"We've heard of *Rendal Hemmons*, Your Grace." Terry practically spat Rendal's name. "We don't want to speak to him. We want to speak to *you*."

Rendal stepped to the chair that was waiting for him. "The Prefect would like you to meet me. Does that not matter?" He pulled the chair out slowly, his wounded side on display for everyone.

When he finally sat, the room was silent, all eyes on him.

"Rendal...speaks...for me," Slidell managed to get out.

"This is lunacy!" a woman toward the far end of the table cried. Her name was Patricia. "This man is a charlatan, and we all know it. We're not going to sit here and listen to him, are we?"

The table's attention turned to her.

Rendal smiled. "Patricia, you should calm down. You don't want your blood pressure to get high. It's not good for your health."

"My... My *blood pressure*?" the woman yelled back.

"Perhaps we can all talk reasonably for a moment?" Rendal looked around the rest of the table. "Tell me why it is you dislike me so much, and perhaps I can help assuage some of your fears?"

"You're kidding, right?" Terry asked. He pointed at the Prefect. "Look at him. That's not our leader. That's not the man in charge of this kingdom. You've *done* something to him."

Rendal turned his head to Slidell, and his eyes narrowed as he studied the man. "Why, you may be right. He *does* look different than when I first showed up. He looks…slower, somehow."

"He mocks us!" Patricia shouted. "In our own meeting quarters, he mocks us!"

"Harold," Rendal called, still feigning concern. "Does this man look different to you?"

"Yes, sir. Very different."

"I won't stand for this!" a third person shouted across the table. His chair flew back as he rose to his feet. "We're going to call for this charlatan's death immediately!"

Rendal's eyes flashed red as he turned to the man. "If you won't stand for it, then please *sit*."

A cracking sound rang through the room. The man let out an agonizing scream and hit the floor with a thud.

His yelling flooded across the room, almost unending.

"Harold," Rendal said, the red in his eyes fading, "would you mind removing Mr. Yensen from the room? He seems to be in serious pain."

"Certainly, sir," Harold answered, already striding across the room. He grabbed the man by the arms and slid him across the floor, the man shouting and begging the whole way.

Rendal smiled at the people who remained seated. "I

just thought it was ironic, ya know? He said 'I won't stand,' but then he stood up. Isn't that kind of silly?"

The table stared at him, all of their eyes wide. A few people's mouths hung open, unable to close.

"Sorry." Rendal shook his head. "What were we speaking about again? You all didn't want to talk to me?"

Patricia's eyes lit red, and Rendal smiled. "Did you not like my demonstration with Mr. Yensen?"

Rendal stood. His eyes were still their normal color. "Before you do something you may regret, we should talk first. I think it'll be in everyone's best interests if we do."

His eyes glowed red as he glanced at her.

"But if you'd rather I crack every bone in your body, then have Harold drag you out of the room, that's fine too. Everything is up to you, dearest ones."

Patricia remained standing, her eyes not fading to their original color.

"Patricia," someone whispered, "sit down. Hear him out." They weren't looking at the woman as they spoke. They were staring at the blood streaks Mr. Yensen had left as Harold pulled him across the floor.

Patricia's eyes faded. She didn't sit, but Rendal didn't care. He let his eyes die down and then took his seat. "Now, let's try to talk like adults, shall we?"

He looked at Slidell. The man stared forward endlessly, a short string of drool hanging from his lower lip.

"He's so messy sometimes!" Rendal laughed, sounding as if he were discussing a young child instead of an adult.

He turned back to the table. "Some of you can use magic. Some of you can't. It doesn't matter. If Patricia down there, or any of the rest of you wants to challenge me, be my guest. You'll end up in worse shape than Mr. Yensen."

Rendal leaned back in his chair, grimacing as he did. "I'd hoped that my wound would help persuade you all that New Perth's threat is real. I'd hoped that I could perhaps..."

Harold walked in, and Rendal looked at him.

"Harold, what is it that I'd hoped to do with this group? I'm having a tough time remembering the word."

"You were hoping to fool them, sir."

"Ah!" Rendal exclaimed in mock surprise. "That's right! I wanted to *fool* you all into believing that we really had spies and war was coming. But then I showed up and... Well, *look* at him." He turned to Slidell. "The Prefect isn't going to be much help."

Rendal shook his head as if disappointed.

"Anyway, I figure the direct approach is always best, so let me be direct. I run this kingdom now. Your Royal Guard lies dead on their training ground, all five of them killed by my hand. The men beneath them will certainly be no match if they wish to test me. My ten ships outside? There are no goods to sell on them. Instead, I brought an army with me. You've probably already seen them. They haven't taken complete control yet, because it's not necessary..."

Rendal grew quiet for a moment.

He stared at them without mercy. "Unless you *make* it necessary. Then all of you will suffer, and the kingdom will suffer more. I don't want that, do I, Harold?"

"No, sir. Not at all," Harold answered dutifully.

"Exactly. We should work as a team—you, me, the Prefect here. That's the only way it's going to end well for all of us, you understand?" Rendal looked behind his chair at Harold. "Will you bring the map, please?"

Harold said nothing but hustled over. He rolled out a large scroll, showing the continent in totality.

On one side, Sidnie was marked. On the other, New Perth.

"Before we get started in earnest," Rendal said, "Are there any questions so far?"

Everyone around the table looked far too shocked to speak.

"Good!" Rendal clapped, smiling broadly. "Let's look at the map, then. Now, as you can see, we're here. And 'they' are there."

Rendal looked around the table, his face grave. "Make no mistake, ladies and gentlemen: we are at war. Perhaps you didn't want it. Perhaps you *don't* want it. That doesn't matter anymore, because it's about to begin. New Perth *does* have spies here."

"Who?" a woman to his left said.

"I'm sure you all know where I got this wound—the demonstration with the spy. Well, the supposed spy was faked, but the man who cut my side open was not. He's New Perth's Right Hand, and while he's the first, he won't be the last. More will come."

"For you, though," Terry interjected. "Not for *us*. Not for *Sidnie*."

Rendal smiled. "What's the difference? I've taken it upon myself to begin preparing us. That's what you've seen with our military and our new magic school."

"*Our?*" Patricia called from the other side of the table.

The mage sighed. "I feel like I'm not getting through to

you. There is no you and me. There is only *our*. Harold, will you tell them?"

"Certainly, sir." Harold remained standing slightly back from the table. "If you all don't support Mr. Hemmons, he's going to kill you. Perhaps publicly. He is growing slightly perturbed with your inability to understand this, as am I."

"Thank you, Harold." Rendal addressed the table again. "Now, are there any questions about *that*? If so, please ask them now, because we have important things to discuss."

"What if we want out?" Patricia asked. She was clearly nervous, her fingers tapping on the table. "If we don't want to oppose you but we don't want to be advisors anymore? We just want to leave, to let you do as you will with this place, but to not include us?"

"Hmmm." Rendal's brow scrunched, and he put his hand to his chin. "You mean... Like, we all go our separate ways? That's what you're talking about?"

Patricia nodded. "Yes. Exactly. Separate ways."

"Hmmm... Harold, what do you think?"

Harold grinned. "Well, on the face of it, it seems like a great idea."

"That's what I was thinking." Rendal stood. "Who would like to leave? Just go their separate way, and leave me to rule the kingdom...with the Prefect of course?"

Four hands rose.

"Any others?" the mage asked.

The other five at the table stared straight forward, not daring to move.

"Okay. Good. You who raised your hands can leave. We will handle Sidnie from here on out." Rendal gestured toward the closed door on the other side of the room.

The four looked at each other, none fully able to believe their good fortune.

"Go on," Rendal urged. "Work to be done and such."

Patricia turned first, and the others followed, making their way toward the door.

Another man stood up. "Can I go with them?"

"Certainly. Separate ways sounds like the best idea." Rendal nodded toward the door with a smile. "Hurry now."

The man caught up with the other four.

"One more thing."

The five stopped walking, quickly turning to look at the mage.

"Ah, never mind. You wouldn't care. Good luck to the five of you."

Patricia only paused for another moment. She obviously wanted out of this man's presence.

She reached the door and pulled the handle. The door swung open.

Three men clad in armor and wearing red necklaces stepped through. Their necklaces weren't lit up, although their faces were focused.

"What's this?" Patricia shrieked.

It was the last thing she ever said.

The three men cut down those trying to leave.

They lay dead on the floor, and the three armored men stepped back out and closed the door behind them.

"I forgot to tell them," Rendal said as he looked back at the rest of the table, "that the guards outside were under strict instructions to kill anyone who walked through if Harold or I weren't with them."

He smiled.

"You all, of course, are free to go, just as they were. Unfortunately, those men out there are still there and have the same instructions."

Terry looked at Rendal. "I'm perfectly fine right where I am."

"That's the spirit, Terry!" Rendal sounded positively gleeful.

"Me too."

"Yeah. No need to go anywhere."

The entire table agreed with Rendal. That was how he'd planned it, of course: agree...or die.

"Now," Rendal began. "The Prefect and I, of course, have great respect for his advisors, those of you remaining. We want to share our plan with you because make no mistake...we're going to conquer New Perth and then the entire continent."

Rendal and Harold stood on the tower's balcony. It circled the entire top of the structure, offering a truly stunning view.

Rendal looked down at the lights below, the wind rushing across his body.

"How many days have we been here, Harold?" he asked.

"Five, sir."

"And in five days, we've conquered the entire kingdom. We've got a military lumbering into action, and a school training mages." Rendal grew quiet as he stared forward.

"Yes, sir. It truly has been awesome to watch," Harold answered.

Rendal turned around, leaning on the railing. "There's more, Harold. I haven't even begun to use my powers yet."

Harold said nothing, only looked at his master.

"Artino...," Rendal mused, looking wistfully up into the air. "The man is a genius. If he had an ounce of ambition besides toiling away in his laboratory, he'd rule the entire world."

Rendal reached into his pocket and pulled out a tiny orb. Green stones exactly like those in the necklaces circled the outside of it in two perpendicular circles.

The orb fit into the palm of his hand.

"This is just a tiny bit of what Artino is creating. Sidnie has a whole host of engineers, and Artino is putting them to work. He tells me they're smart enough people, and once he showed them his plans, they started replicating it en masse."

Harold stared at the small globe. "What is it, sir?"

"An explosive. Given Sidnie's reliance on magic, they've spent a lot of resources finding amphoralds beneath the ground. They have entire warehouses full of the things, and Artino is making full use of them. That's what makes this explosive possible."

"Excuse me, sir?" Harold asked, unable to take his eyes away from the tiny black orb.

"Think about a bomb, only much smaller." Rendal looked down at the object too. "There are mechanisms inside it that will inflict fire and pain on anyone near it. He's creating thousands of these things, some larger."

"Won't that destroy New Perth, sir?" Harold asked.

"It depends," the mage responded. "If I use them directly over the kingdom, yes. They could very well demolish the place. I only plan on doing that in a desperate situation, however."

"Sir, if I may ask, where do you plan on using them, then?"

"Here, Harold. There are huge swaths of this kingdom that house only the indigent." Rendal turned around so his back was to Harold. He looked out at the kingdom once again. "These are a deterrent, Harold. I'm going to use them against Riley. Very soon she's going to see how little I care about the lives of others. They are expendable. They all serve a greater purpose."

Harold nodded, although remained silent.

"I'm concerned with what happened when you met William," the mage commented. "I thought you could handle him, Harold."

The head guard frowned. "I can, sir."

A light tone of mockery underlaid Rendal's voice. "Is that what you call what I saw? My side is *still* healing, and from what I can tell, the Right Hand raced off across into the kingdom. Tell me, am I wrong about any of this?"

"No, sir."

Rendal nodded. "No, I didn't fucking *think* so." Anger ripped through Rendal's voice. "You're an important part of this, Harold, as long as you prove beneficial to the end goal. If you can't, there are people I can replace you with."

Rendal turned around and looked at his head guard.

"Tell me, how do you plan on stopping this Right Hand? He has the ability to use magic and you don't. What are you going to do?"

Harold matched the mage's gaze. "Use those."

"Use what?" Rendal asked.

"That little orb in your pocket."

Rendal's still face slowly spread into a grin. "That's good thinking, Harold, but it won't work. The explosive triggers are *inside* the device. You have to use magic to operate them."

Harold nodded but didn't look away. "If Artino is the genius you say he is, it shouldn't be much of a problem to put the trigger outside."

Rendal's grin turned into an out-and-out smile. "Oh, Harold, perhaps *you're* the genius. I'm sure Artino could do that for a brother-in-arms; certainly for one as important as you." Rendal reached into his pocket and pulled out the black orb once again. Looking at it and still beaming, he said, "You warm my heart with your devious ways. I think the next time William shows up, he's going to be in for a big surprise."

CHAPTER FOUR

"Y ou're so slow, Worth." Riley grinned as she spoke. "If it wasn't for you, I'd already be in Sidnie."

"If not for Worth, you be dead. Lucky Worth slow you down," the tent leader responded.

Riley kept on, ignoring his comment. "I mean, I could basically *fly* there. Just use my sword and catapult myself into the air. Land, and do it all over again. But no, with *you* here, I have to ride this damn camel. It's really cumbersome."

Worth took the pack off his back. He'd been working on a new contraption to help him drink wine, and Riley was actually impressed with it. He didn't need to open the pack anymore and dip a chalice into it.

Instead, he had a straw that he'd sealed with wax poking from a hole he'd cut in the top. He simply put his mouth to it and sucked, the paper straw turning purple as wine moved up it.

When he finished, he put the pack on his back and said, "Worth break your sword. Then you ride camel forever.

Camel not like you either. Told me last night. Said you smell bad."

Riley grinned. She glanced at Eric, who was grinning as well. The three of them were riding behind Thomas, his camel in the lead. They'd been riding for two days, sleeping a few hours each night before waking and starting again.

Riley was keeping them at a grueling pace, but no one had said anything so far. Thomas wouldn't, because he worshipped the ground Riley walked on. Eric was young and strong, and more, he thought of Riley as his mentor. He wouldn't want to disappoint her.

And Worth?

Well, the lovable bastard was stubborn.

"Savior," Thomas called from up front. "May I have a word?"

"Ha!" Worth laughed. "He funny, huh, Eric?"

Eric said nothing, only grinned at the bald man's jesting.

"Thomas, *please* call me Riley. There's no need for 'Savior' or anything else resembling it," Riley told their guide.

"I apologize, Riley," Thomas responded. "I cannot promise that it won't happen again."

Riley sighed, knowing that Worth was going to pick at her about it. This shit better end before they got to William or Riley would never hear the end of it. "What's going on, Thomas?"

"I thought you might want to know that there are raiders ahead. I don't *think* they've spotted us; their attention is on a piece of a caravan that's been separated from the rest."

Riley closed her eyes, feeling the camel rocking beneath

her as it walked forward. She tried to reach out and see what Thomas did, but wasn't able to. She saw only darkness.

She was mastering other areas of magic, but the Psychic kind was still beyond her.

Riley opened her eyes. "Are they out of our way?"

"Some, yes."

She sighed. She needed to get to Sidnie above all else. Her friends needed *her*. Mason needed her.

But what would Mason say if she skipped out on helping the innocent in order to save him?

"Also," Thomas interrupted her thoughts. "I think they can use magic."

"Ha!" Worth shouted again. "Told you. Told *all* of you. Worth said we leave, we going to die."

He was grinning widely, his lips purple. He was either kidding, or the sun was making him lose his mind; Riley couldn't tell which.

"Thomas, is there any way we can send Worth to fight them alone while we wait here? Maybe build a tent to keep us out of the sun?"

Thomas turned around on his camel, his eyes narrowed and his face serious. He nodded slowly. "It's possible."

Riley tried to hide her grin. She needed to remember that these people thought she was a god of some sort, and would literally do anything she asked—including sacrificing Worth to raiders while they rested.

"I'm just joking, Thomas. Let's go see what we can do to help these people. How many raiders are there?" Riley asked.

"Ten to twenty. It's hard for me to tell."

"Worth, can you see any more?" Riley said to the tent man.

"Worth see everything, but Worth not tell Riley. She mean." He winked.

Riley knew that was his way of saying no. Another reason she chose Thomas was that he possessed some of the strongest Psychic magic of the Chosen. If *he* couldn't tell, Worth wouldn't be able to.

"The only thing Worth sees clearly is the bottom of a bottle so he knows when to buy more," Riley jested before turning her attention to Thomas. "Let's get there as quickly as we can."

"Yes, my Savior," Thomas responded.

Riley shook her head and caught Worth chuckling out of the corner of her eye.

The camels walked onward, with Thomas veering their path to the north some.

The sun beat down as the crew rode in silence. Riley kept trying to focus her mind, to see the raiders up ahead. It was no use; she couldn't reach that part of her magic.

Riley's eyes caught the raiders before anyone else. "That's them."

"I can't see them yet, my Savior," Thomas answered. "Only with my mind."

"Eric, can you?" Riley asked.

"I think so. I'm not sure."

"Worth, I'm sure you're too drunk to see anything farther than five feet in front of your camel," Riley joked.

"Worth see everything, all time. You wish you have Worth eyes." The man's lips were purple, but he wasn't wobbling on his saddle. Riley thought he might actually be able to outdrink William.

They rode a bit farther. "See them yet?" Riley asked.

Everyone nodded their affirmation.

And how could they miss it? The part of the caravan that had been broken off from the larger group was in flames. Riley saw two wagons, one of them on fire. People were strewn across the ground; Riley couldn't tell if they were dead.

The raiders were much closer in number to twenty than ten.

"We've got to hurry," Riley whispered, her mind snapping into warrior mode.

They were still a half mile away, but the raiders saw them now. They were walking away from the caravan, forming a line as they peered at the coming strangers.

"Oh, you so fast," Worth interjected. "You go. Hurry now, Queen of Questions." He grinned.

Riley looked at him. "Same bet William and I make?"

"What bet?"

"I kill more than you," Riley answered.

"I'll kill more than both of you," Eric snapped with a wild smile. He spurred the camel beneath him, and the creature bolted forward, heading across the expanse and leaving the others in the dust.

"He cheat!" Worth cried as he kicked his own camel.

Everyone raced across the sand, and Riley kept her eyes on the raiders. They understood what was happening now: the raiders were about to be raided.

"To the right!" Riley shouted, sensing the coming wind before anyone else.

Sand was blowing toward them, and Riley saw the perpetrator—a woman standing in the center of the raiders' line, her eyes bright red.

Worth saw the same, and he raised his hand up in a sweeping gesture from his waist to above his shoulder.

The sandstorm slammed into an invisible barrier, millions of tiny specks scattering across an unseen wall.

Eric was still in front, and Riley knew she wouldn't beat him there on the camel. She wanted to win this damned bet.

Riley stood up in her saddle, then placed one foot on the camel's back, carefully steadying herself.

Her eyes lit up as she unsheathed her sword.

She touched it lightly to the leather saddle, and at the same time pushed down with her legs, her focus on reaching the raiders before anyone else.

Riley leapt into the air, soaring through space and passing everyone beneath her.

She looked down at the rapists and murderers, four of their pairs of eyes red now as they stared up at her.

She hit the ground with one knee down and sand billowed out from her landing place, smashing into the raiders running for her. The tiny specks of sand flew with such force that they sliced her enemies' flesh, creating strips of red across their faces and arms.

Riley looked up, still on one knee.

She was immediately able to tell that some of the tent people were dead, but not all of them.

"Care to fuck with someone who can fight back?" she asked as the sand fell away.

The raiders had stopped running and were now staring with real fear at the person in front of them.

"She's just a girl!" someone shouted. "And a hot one at that! I'll take her over the trash back there!"

Riley smiled. She was going to love this, and everyone else was still a quarter mile away.

She stood.

The raiders rushed toward her.

Riley threw her sword forward while she remained in place.

She closed her eyes, not worrying about the possible death coming for her.

Riley focused on the sword, directing it as she willed. She saw it slicing through the raiders, cutting their necks and stomachs, severing spines.

She felt heat; some form of fire rushing toward her.

Water, she thought—the first time such a *magic* idea had occurred to her.

She brought her arms up, palms facing outward, and spread them to the right and left.

A shield of water manifested from the air. Riley opened her eyes and watched the fireball slam into it. The water sizzled and steam rose into the air, the shield bending as the fireball tried to force its way through.

Riley didn't budge. She watched as the water extinguished the flames.

She dropped her hands to the side, the shield falling to the ground.

Men and women lay dead in front of her, only a few left.

"Please. Please don't kill me," a man in front of her begged.

His eyes were red, though. Riley knew he was begging for time, not his life. He would attack the moment he thought he could get away with it.

"The people behind you," Riley said. "Did they beg you to let them live?"

The man shook his head quickly, but Riley saw the truth on his face.

He threw his hands forward, hoping to get a fireball out of them in time, but for the raider, there was no more time.

Riley's sword, floating in the air behind him, plunged into his back.

His red eyes faded and his hands fell to his sides.

He collapsed face-first into the sand.

Riley turned and looked at the three now arriving. Her sword removed itself from the dead raider and floated through the air to Riley's open hand. She grasped it, feeling complete as she did.

"Glad you could make it." She grinned as her eyes turned to their usual color.

"Damn it, Riley." Eric dismounted his camel, looking at the group of dead behind her. "You couldn't save me a couple?"

"You cheat." Worth landed with a thud on the sand.

"Well done, my Savior," Thomas commented, remaining on his camel.

Riley turned around to look at the caravan's damage.

"Thank you," a woman whispered. She was hiding behind a camel but peeking her head out at Riley from the other side of the burning wagon.

"I'm sorry we were not faster," Riley responded. She looked at the dead tent people, tears coming to her eyes. "Truly. I'm sorry."

People started climbing out of the wagon that wasn't on fire.

"A lot more of us could have died." The woman stepped out from behind the camel now, revealing herself fully. "You made sure that didn't happen."

"She just want all credit," Worth interjected. He took his backpack off and sucked down a large gulp of wine.

"Ignore him, please." Riley's eyes were kind. "I'm sorry for those I couldn't save. Will you be able to make it back to the rest of the caravan?"

The woman nodded. "We should. The raiders used their magic to confuse us and the rest of the caravan. That was how they separated us. Now that they're gone, we should be able to find our way."

Riley looked at the dead raiders. "They got what they deserved. When I return to New Perth, I promise I'll work toward putting a stop to this. It's sickening."

She meant it, too. Riley was coming to realize that the world outside of New Perth wasn't nearly as safe as hers. That though the innocent survived and thrived inside her kingdom, the people who lived beyond its walls didn't fare so well. They needed help.

She couldn't do anything about it now, though, or no more than what she'd just done. "I wish you well, you and your family."

"Thank you," the woman answered.

Riley turned and looked at Thomas. "We have to continue forward."

"Of course, my Savior."

"It go to her head." Worth put his hands around his own head and started expanding them. "Make her think she better than she is. Arrogant."

Riley darted her sword toward Worth playfully, and he dodged it easily. Half in the bag, Worth was still agile.

"Come on, ya lazy jokers. Let's get moving," Riley ordered with a grin.

Riley watched Worth, who was sitting away from the campsite. The fire's light didn't reach that far, so Worth was alone with only the moon to shine on him.

He had his feet folded beneath him again but no wine anywhere around.

Riley stood from the fire and walked across the sand, leaving Eric and Thomas. The fire was dying, and they were nearing sleep anyway. They'd reach Sidnie tomorrow evening, so Riley wanted them to rest as much as they could right now.

She didn't know what to expect when they got to the kingdom, but exhaustion wouldn't help anyone.

She reached Worth, but he didn't look over. He kept staring forward as if there were something to see in the darkness beyond.

"Are you looking at them?" Riley asked.

"You. Too many questions. Why you no sleep?" He didn't look up as he spoke.

"Because I need to know what's going on and you're the only one who can tell me."

"Worth no want tell. You go away. Leave Worth alone." The bald man's face was neither smiling nor cross, but rather lax as he looked forward.

"You're watching them now, aren't you?"

Worth nodded.

Riley sat next to the tent man. "Tell me what you see."

He finally looked at her, and his eyes narrowed. "You *could* see if not impatient. You..." He shook his head. "You *impatient.*"

"They're all I have, Worth. They're everything in this world to me. You have to understand that." Riley didn't want to fight about this. They were here, and there wasn't anything they could do about it now. A day away from their destination, and they could only go forward.

Worth nodded and looked at the dark sand in front of him. "I see them, yes."

"What are they doing?"

"What they said they would," Worth answered. "They understanding what mage do."

"How's William?"

Worth closed his eyes. "Can't *see* with all these *questions.*"

"Then stop looking and talk to me. I need to know how he is." Riley scooted around so that she sat directly in front of Worth, giving him no place to look but at her.

"He...hurt, but okay. He fine."

"Hurt?" Riley's anxiety rose immediately.

"A little. Not much," Worth answered, his eyes still closed.

"How?"

He shook his head. "This why Worth no answer. One

question leads to more. You never stop." He opened his eyes. "He saved child. Fought mage."

"A child?"

Worth threw his hands in the air and Riley couldn't help but smile. "Your frustration is endearing, Worth."

"Frustration make Worth throw *you*."

"Okay. No child questions, but William is okay?"

Worth sighed and nodded. "He lost sword, but okay, yes."

Riley wanted to ask about the sword, but she understood Worth would only grow angrier. She needed to know about everyone else. "Lucie, Erin, Verith? They're all okay?"

"Okay... Yes. Danger, but okay."

"Danger?" Riley asked.

"Mage strong. He... He own kingdom now—"

Riley gasped. "The whole thing?"

Worth nodded again. "Whole thing."

"It's only been a few *days*. How is that possible?"

"You don't listen. Poor student. Stubborn. He *strong*." Worth looked like he wanted to throttle Riley.

She didn't care. "He's always been strong, but I'm strong now, too. We'll stop him. All I need to know is that my friends are safe. If they're okay, then *we're* okay."

"They okay," Worth answered.

Riley stood up. "Maybe it's you who's stubborn."

Worth raised his eyebrows. "Worth?"

"You're not listening to me," Riley explained. "That I'm going to beat him. That I'm going to stop him."

Worth chuckled. "Me stubborn? That what Riley think?"

"More stubborn than me, certainly." Riley grinned. "Especially if you don't think I can beat Rendal's ass."

"Mayhap you can." Worth nodded. "Mayhap."

"No mayhap to it, you lush. I can and will. When I get to that kingdom, I'm going to show you."

Worth was smiling now, and that made Riley feel better.

"Let's bet, aye?" he asked.

"Bet what?"

"That you no kick ass...yet." Worth looked at her, grinning.

"Okay. What's the wager?" Riley asked.

"If you lose, Worth..." He paused for a moment, peering at the sand while he thought. His smile blossomed on his face again, growing wide. "If you lose, you Worth servant for one week, aye?"

Riley grinned back at him. "And if I'm right, you're *my* servant for a week?"

"Aye, but you not right. *Worth* right. You see."

Riley extended her hand to the bald man. "You got yourself a bet, Worth. I hope you like doing laundry."

Worth's eyes narrowed, and he threw one leg out in front of him. "Worth need toenails cut. First job for Riley."

He started laughing, and the Right Hand couldn't help but join in.

Evening fell around the group as they looked at the mighty kingdom.

"Mighty" was the only word that fit.

Riley was agape.

"I've never seen anything so great," she told everyone and no one.

"Aye," Worth agreed. "And he own all."

"Rendal?" Eric asked.

Worth nodded. "Aye. Those lights. His. Those buildings. His. All Sidnie now his."

Riley knew what the tent man was trying to do—scare her into leaving. What he said was true, she knew that, but she also knew what he thought about her.

She wasn't ready.

"Worth, if you don't quit trying to frighten me, you're going to end up with a sword sticking out of your skull."

"All talk." Worth grinned. "Can't drink wine like Worth, can't fight like Worth."

They stood a half-mile from the massive stone gates that let travelers in and out of the kingdom. There were guards at it, but the gates stood open. Even now, as the sun descended, people were coming and going.

Small vendors sat to both the left and right of the entrance, still not packed up for the day.

"My Savior, do you want to just go straight in?" Thomas asked.

Riley was studying the guards. Sentries walked atop the walls, and a few archers remained in the battlements.

She didn't see anyone wearing red necklaces, although that didn't mean a whole lot.

"Thoughts, Worth?" she said.

"Worth think we leave now. Go back to underground people. Learn."

"The *Chosen*," Thomas corrected with a sigh. It didn't

matter how hard he tried, Worth was never going to stop with the "underground people" moniker.

"Yeah, yeah. Chosen live under ground. That what you chosen." Worth laughed. "If Riley want be dumb, we go straight through gates. Worth no think they look."

"What's this imbecile saying, my Savior?" Thomas looked at Riley as if they both understood how horrible it was traveling with such an idiot.

"Never mind, the both of you," Riley responded with a grin. "We'll go through the gates. Eric, you ready?"

"Aye, my Savior." He was grinning too, mocking Thomas as well as Worth.

When Riley gave him a sideways glance he fought the grin away, but only barely.

She started her camel forward. She hadn't named it officially yet, but the animal was a good one. He would never be as personal as her horse Wind Whisper, but she still liked him.

"Hey, Worth," she called as their animals moved toward the gates. "Did you name your camel?"

"Aye. Name Riley. So stubborn."

Riley shook her head, laughing, and said nothing else.

They reached the gates, and the guards didn't give her a glance.

They went through without being asked for identification or anything else.

"A trusting kingdom," she whispered.

"Aye. Maybe it want you here," Worth responded as his camel caught up to hers. "Maybe kingdom want you inside."

"Well, it got what it wanted if that's the case. Now where do we go?"

The four of them stood in a line looking at the massive structures before them. Buildings. Huge roads going left and right, then crossing over and over.

"You ask Worth?" He turned his head, his eyebrows going up. "How Worth know? Worth say no come here. You stubborn. No listen."

"It never ends," Thomas said.

"No. It end. Worth go find wine. I find them too. You hide. See you soon. Goodbye, lovelies." He smiled, spurred his camel, and took off.

"He's joking, right?" Eric asked.

"Nope." Riley shook her head. "He's going to get drunk and possibly find them."

"What if something happens to him?" Eric looked honestly troubled.

"I'd be more worried about something happening to his wine. I pity the person who spills it. *He'll* be fine." Riley looked away from Worth. "Thomas, it's your turn to deliver what Alexandra said you could. Take us to our connections."

Rendal quit speaking mid-sentence. He stared out the window in front of him, his eyes growing wider.

"Sir, is everything okay?" Harold asked.

Rendal's mouth opened as if he wanted to say something, but no words came out.

"What is it, Rendal?" Mason questioned from the couch.

It was the first time the Assistant Prefect had spoken in hours, but even he noticed the definite change in the mage's demeanor.

Rendal turned around and looked at the Assistant Prefect. "She's here, Mason."

"Riley?"

"That's right. The one and only." Rendal's eyes were bright, though not flaming red. Energy ran through his body as if a bolt of lightning had hit him.

"You can feel her, sir?" Harold asked.

Rendal grimaced. "It's different than last time. *She's* different."

"How?" Mason stood up from the couch.

Rendal slowly raised his head, a smile on his face that sent chills across Mason. "Someone taught her magic. She's a mage now."

Lucie had remained in the background during each step of this shadow war with Rendal and his growing power. She'd first left New Perth to venture north, only wanting to see if it was possible. If the mage she'd once loved had somehow been siphoning off people's magic potential.

She'd seen it was true, and been thrown in a cage as if the two had never been lovers.

Lucie ventured out again and joined a ship, following Riley after the Assistant Prefect.

She'd only voiced her opinion a few times, and in the end, she'd been overruled.

Lucie was comfortable in the background. She was comfortable ribbing William whenever the chance arose.

But there were things to be done as well. Things that no one else *could* do—at least not in this group.

Because she knew Riley. Of course, William did too, but he was engaged elsewhere right now. His mind was on getting to *Rendal*, so he'd lost his focus on Riley.

Lucie knew Riley would be concentrating on the exact same thing.

Riley had left to go learn how to release her magic, but how long would she remain away?

Lucie didn't think Riley would—nay, *could*—stay away for any length of time. Lucie had known the girl, and now she knew the woman, and the thirst for Justice was in her.

That thirst would drive her to Sidnie. Lucie thought one of two things would happen, both simple. Riley would or would not learn to loose the magic inside her, but either way, she was coming to Sidnie.

So Lucie remained in the background, but she was constantly looking for the Right Hand.

She would show, and Lucie had to find her before Rendal did.

Night was upon the kingdom now, both Brighten and Erin at their respective "jobs."

The others were napping, as they did every night before those two returned.

Lucie had been slipping out in the short hours of quiet that dominated their adopted home. She didn't want anyone knowing about it because she needed to move in stealth, and the fewer people who knew, the fewer who could talk.

The house had two doors, a front and a back.

Lucie looked around the main room they all slept in. It was dark, with little light making its way in. She heard the familiar sounds of light snores and deep breathing.

Lucie stepped through the room without a sound. She wasn't doing anything *wrong*, of course, but there was a *wrong* way to do it: telling anyone she was doing anything at all.

The house's back door was little more than a tarp thrown over a hole. Lucie pushed it out of the way and stepped through.

A hulking giant stood two feet in front of her.

Her eyes flashed red, and fire blazed from her hands.

"Easy, old lady," William whispered. "Easy, now. You don't want to burn me to a crisp. You'll have no one to badger with your witless jokes."

"Father in the sky, William!" Lucie's voice was harsh but still a whisper. "You almost just got yourself killed."

"You couldn't kill me if I was hogtied and you had twenty minutes." The moon showed him smiling slightly. "Now, where you been goin' these past few nights?"

"Why you followin' me, William? That's the real question. I'm a grown woman damn near twice your age, and I'll go where I please." She stepped forward, ready to walk around him.

William's arm shot out and blocked her path, although he was careful not to touch her.

"Twice my age is right, and walkin' so late at night, ya might trip and break a hip, old lady." He was still grinning, her mock anger at being followed affecting him not one bit. "Now, tell me where it is you're heading off to. I don't think ya got a fling around these parts, and the Prefect help me if you're out trying to rekindle a romance with Rendal—"

"Hush your mouth before you lose your tongue, boy," Lucie spat.

William chuckled. "I'm kiddin', Lucie, but you need to tell me the truth. I've been watchin' you leave every night, thinkin' you were sneakin' through that damned room like some kinda trained spy. Woman, I'm a Right Hand. I may talk brash and walk brash, but nothin' gets by me. I've been watching you leave and come back when you thought everyone was still sleepin'."

He gestured with his head back to the room.

"I imagine Verith might have a clue, too. He's no slouch. I suppose I coulda just followed you, but that woulda seemed wrong, too. I'd rather talk to you about it like equals."

William stared her dead in the eye.

"Now, old lady, where ya goin'?"

Lucie relaxed some and looked away from the giant. Her eyes went to the other shitty houses surrounding them; this place wasn't a slum, but it was only about a half step above one. She couldn't put William off anymore, and she knew it.

He was right. They were in this together. There were no separate teams.

"I'm lookin' for Riley," she whispered as if someone in the house might hear her.

"That's what I figured was happening. You think she's coming here, don't you? Already?"

Lucie nodded. "That was the plan since the beginning,

and I don't think she's gonna be able to keep away for long, so I've been lookin' for her at night."

William chuckled and turned so they both faced the crumbling buildings. "How you plan on findin' her, Lucie? Just wandering around until you run into her?"

"When the creators gave out brains, they skipped you, William. I've heard that the creators went back a second time, because they had more brains left, but they must have forgotten all about you on that round too." She shook her head. "*No.* I'm not wandering around hoping I run into her."

"So, old and wise one, tell me what you're doin' then," William demanded.

"I'm usin' magic, ya dolt. I'm looking through the kingdom to see if she's hiding, but I can't do it from inside this house. There's too many people, and the kingdom is too big."

William nodded. "I'mma need Worth to teach me that kinda magic."

"Don't matter what he teaches you. You're too dumb to get it." Lucie allowed herself to crack a smile.

"Yeah, yeah. I hope Riley ain't back yet. You two plus Kris is gonna make me end up hurtin' one of you." William stepped onto the tiny dirt patch in front of them. "Come on, let's go."

"You're not goin'." Lucie's head snapped up. "You'll get us both caught, your big feet clogging around everywhere. You're a *wanted man*, William, in case you forgot."

"Two things, old lady," William explained. "The first is, if somethin' happens, you ain't gonna be able to protect yourself. Magic or no magic, a group falls on you and *they* have magic, you're gonna need help. The second is, if Riley is lookin' for someone, who do ya think *she's* lookin' for? Me, not some old hag in a hood."

Lucie raised her foot and stomped on William's toe.

"OW!"

"Handle myself just fine, moron, but I'm tired of sittin' out here arguin' with you about this nonsense. If you're comin', try not to get us caught."

Lucie walked forward, not caring if William followed.

She started down the usual streets, heading out of the slums toward the more populated parts of the kingdom. William caught up with her easily enough by taking long strides.

"Where ya been lookin'?" he whispered.

"I've been making my rounds at the smaller lodgings," Lucie answered without looking at him. They were just about to cross from their neighborhood into the kingdom proper.

"That might not be the best way, you know." He smiled as he spoke, clearly thinking he was being more clever than Lucie.

"What's the *best* way, William?"

"You're lookin' for the wrong one."

"What the hell ya talkin' about?" Lucie asked, stopping at the corner of the road and whipping around to him.

"You're lookin' for Riley, but it's gonna be hard to find her if she ain't lookin' for you. Sure, you can use your magic, but Riley might not know how to show a beacon. You know who would?"

Understanding came to Lucie then. "William, this may be the one and only smart thing you've ever said."

"Now that's a damned lie, but I ain't gonna hold it against you, because I know my intellect bests yours." He was smiling broadly. "Worth is who we should be lookin' for because he'll be the one lookin' for us. Or at least using a magic beacon or whatever the hell he'd call it."

"He'd be with Riley, though," Lucie commented.

William shook his head, pretending exasperation as if he couldn't *believe* how dumb Lucie was.

"I'm gonna burn you black as toast," she told him. "Just get it out and let's get movin'."

"It's just tough, Lucie," William complained, still faking exasperation. "Always having to educate you and such. Worth ain't gonna be sittin' in no lodge. He's goin' to be at a bar. That's where we'll find him, and if we do, he'll take us to Riley sure enough."

Lucie wanted to say something sharp back, but she realized the Right Hand was right. Worth would be where they poured wine, not hiding.

"Let's go," was all she managed as she took off.

William barely managed to contain his laughter, not wanting the whole kingdom to hear him. He followed, pulling his hood over his head.

The two walked the dark streets, and as they grew closer to the business districts, more people started filling the streets. Drunks mainly, but there were guards as well.

"There's more guards," Lucie whispered as they passed an open shop on their right.

"Since when?"

"Since last night," she answered. "There weren't nearly this many before."

That was the truth. She saw one on almost every corner.

"You weren't in this part of town last night," William commented. "Could be it's always like this."

"Maybe," Lucie answered. "Maybe not. Maybe something has changed. I need to find a place these guards aren't. My eyes are gonna change when I start lookin' for him."

"It's Sidnie. Plenty of people use magic here. That shouldn't be a problem." William was walking on her right, his large shoulders not letting anyone else stay on the sidewalk.

"Everything right now is a problem, lout. Even you bein' so big. Goodness, I can't believe I let you come with me. They're gonna see us for sure." Lucie shook her head. "Either way, I'm not using magic where they can see me. Neither of us needs *any* extra scrutiny. So just help me find a damned place to hide."

William grabbed her elbow and pulled her to a stop, and she turned. The big man was smiling.

"I don't think we're gonna need magic to find Worth." He nodded toward an alehouse across the street.

The doors were open, and Lucie be damned, Worth was on the bar. His shirt was off, and sweat dripping down his face and chest.

He was dancing.

His lips were the most purple Lucie had ever seen them. The man was *blitzed*.

William started laughing. "Oh, this is too good. We don't need to go get him. Let's just watch."

Lucie felt the same, although she knew it was the wrong

move. The man was moving across the bar with people actually throwing money at him. He was twisting and turning, playing to the crowd.

The music was loud enough to make its way across the street.

"He's actually got fuckin' rhythm," William said between guffaws.

"We've got to retrieve him," Lucie remarked, finally coming to her senses. "He's going to get himself thrown in jail for indecent exposure. Rendal knows him too. If the guards are lookin' for someone of his description, he's doing an excellent job of helping 'em."

Lucie glanced around quickly. The guards on the road weren't looking at her, but at the drunk man in the bar across the street.

Her eyes turned red briefly while she shot a message to Worth.

Get outside, ya drunk! You're gonna get yourself arrested!

Worth didn't stop dancing, although he did look at her. He winked, his grin as wide as a barn door.

"Oh damn it," Lucie cursed. "He ain't comin' out."

"The hell ya mean, he ain't?" William looked at her.

"I mean, I just sent him a message and he winked at me. The bastard *winked.*"

"Tell him again," William grumbled.

Lucie sent one more message, her eyes flaring red. *Get your ass out here, Worth! We don't have time for this!*

If he was in Sidnie, Riley was here, too. They had to get to her before Rendal did.

Worth didn't even glance at them this time, only turned his ass to them and started shaking it.

"Thank the Mother he's got fuckin' trousers on," Lucie grated.

"I'm gonna beat his fucking thing," William interjected. "We're out here riskin' our damned lives and he's in there livin' it up."

Someone lifted a glass of wine up to Worth. He grabbed it and drained it in seconds.

"We're gonna have to go get him." Lucie sighed.

"Yeah. Definitely *now*. Look."

And sure enough, the guards had had enough. They were moving toward the bar, ready to arrest the drunk who was venturing into the territory of indecent exposure.

"You don't even have a damned sword," Lucie said.

"I can do more damage with my pinky than you can with all the weapons in the world, old lady. Watch and learn."

The guards were moving faster now, pulling out clubs from their belts. They were planning on beating Worth up pretty badly if he didn't listen, and busting him out of jail would be nearly impossible. They had to get him now.

"Sonofabitch!" Lucie whispered harshly.

William started across the street, his hood up. Lucie followed him. Six guards were entering the bar, with more coming from farther down the road. The commotion brought them like moths to a candle.

The crowd paid no mind to any of them, too enraptured with the drunken purple-mouthed man dancing in front of them.

The guards started shoving people out of the way.

"Hey!"

"Watch it!"

People were shouting, realizing everything wasn't fun and games now.

One of the guards brought his club down *hard* on someone's skull.

The man fell like a sack of flour.

The music—a few people in the back playing instruments—stopped.

"You, get down. Get your fuckin' clothes on. You're under arrest."

William entered the bar first, his wide body causing people to stare.

Worth didn't look at Lucie or the Right Hand but kept his eyes on the guards.

"Worth no go with you. Worth drink more!" he shouted, laughing as he did.

He turned around and dropped his pants, his ass hanging out for everyone to see.

A guard swung his club, catching Worth in the back of his leg.

"OWW!" Worth cried, jumping forward as he pulled his pants up. He turned around and looked for the offending party.

"Get the fuck down," the guard who had hit him commanded. "Or there's more where that came from."

Worth hopped down from the bar, his chest still bare.

The crowd was spreading out now, some leaving, others just pushing back toward the walls—giving the bald man and the guards any and all space they needed.

Worth didn't even glance at Lucie and William. To Lucie, he looked flat-out drunk. Perhaps he'd already forgotten they were there.

The guards circled him, but Worth didn't take his eyes off the one who'd hit him. His eyes hadn't turned red, at least.

"Hands behind your back," a guard commanded.

"Worth want wine. And person hit me. Come." He waved his hand in a taunting gesture toward the guard who had used the club, waving him forward.

Someone came from behind, bringing another club down upon Worth's back.

Worth grunted loudly and collapsed to his knees. He kept his head up though, pain bright in his eyes.

"Fuck it." William removed the hood and cloak covering him. He stepped forward, people moving out of his way as if he were a massive wave ready to demolish them. "I believe y'all been lookin' for me?"

The guards all turned, forgetting the bald man on his knee, They looked at the huge warrior taking up much of the establishment.

"Oh, shit!" one of them cried. "It's him! It's the damned spy!"

"No!" Worth shouted, regaining his feet. "Whoever hit Worth, fight now!"

The guards paid him no mind, moving toward William. Lucie moved to the left, blending in with the crowd except for her glowing red eyes.

William's eyes remained normal but he squared up, his fists in front of his face. "Who's first?"

Without a sword, Lucie knew he was going to need help. She also knew why he wasn't using magic. If these guards could use it, he didn't want to provoke them.

She'd be responsible for magic, and hopefully Worth would be smart enough to keep his at bay.

The first man moved on William, swinging the club with both hands. William didn't even try to move, he simply *grabbed* the weapon, wrenching it free of the man's hands.

The guard stood there stunned for a moment. William didn't waste any time, knocking him out cold with a single swing.

He hit the floor.

"One down, five left." He looked at Worth behind the line of men. "You just gonna stand there, baldy?"

Worth grinned.

The two moved, one going left, one going right. They attacked the soldiers as if they'd planned it beforehand. Worth clapped his hands over one man's ears, jarring him before breaking his knee with a brutal stomp.

The man screamed as William bashed two guards' heads together, sending them to the ground.

Lucie looked at the open doors. More guards were just outside, running full speed and ready to take on William and Worth.

Lucie used her magic to slam the alehouse's doors shut.

The first guard slammed straight into them, most likely breaking his nose—though Lucie couldn't see from her vantage point. The others were banging on it, but Lucie bore down with her concentration.

"Boys!" she shouted, "we've got to hurry!"

"Take my time when I fight!" William yelled back. He grabbed a man by the throat and threw him across the room, smashing a chair to smithereens when the man crashed into it.

One guard was now left holding his black club. It shook as he looked at William and Worth, both much larger than him.

William grew very still and leaned forward.

"Boo!"

The guard jumped, then turned and fled, heading through the crowd toward the back entrance.

Worth and William glanced at each other. Worth was slightly bent over from the blows he'd taken, but he was grinning wildly.

"You're a damned drunk, ya know that, tent man?"

"Worth need wine."

William laughed. "Get the man some fuckin' wine!"

The whole place roared with laughter. Only Lucie remained silent, holding the door closed, her eyes a bright red. "You dumbasses aren't listening! We've got to move! At least ten more men are on the other side of that door!"

The bartender was pouring from a jug of wine, ready to give the fresh glass to Worth.

The bald man grabbed the jug out of his hand as if he hadn't been drinking for hours. The bartender had no time to stop him.

"Lehh go!" Worth shouted, his voice finally slurring some.

William went first, heading toward the back. Once again, the crowd moved aside for him, having no other choice besides being mowed down.

The three pushed through the crowd and nearly fell out

the back door, with Worth bringing up the rear. He stumbled into the alley laughing.

"That fun! Again! Again!"

"Damn it, I ain't never seen him this drunk." William turned around to find Lucie standing there. Her eyes were still red.

"I'm holdin' 'em off, but I can't keep doing it for long. They'll be coming down this alley soon if they ain't already headin' for it."

William whipped around and looked at Worth. The tent man had the jug up to his lips, just about ready to take a swig. He smiled as he caught William's eyes.

"What you want, big man? You want Riley, aye?"

"Aye, of course I do. Take us to her," William commanded.

Worth nodded, turned the jug up a bit more and took his drink. He brought it back down and offered it to William. "Go on. Worth know you thirsty."

William smiled, took the jug, and turned it up too.

"You damned drunks are gonna get us killed!" Lucie shouted. "Let's go! Now!"

She shoved both of them in the back, using the strength she made in years of running a restaurant. Despite their size, they launched down the alley, laughing as they went.

"Drink!" Worth reached for the jug. William gave it to him, and the three started running.

"I wish you and Riley would have stayed away," Lucie mumbled as she pulled her hood over her head. They fled down the alley, hanging a left, then taking another. Worth was leading the way, but Lucie didn't know if he could even see straight.

Finally, they ran out onto another packed street, this one busier than the last.

The three drew to a stop, lungs heaving.

"We get rid of 'em?" William asked.

Lucie nodded. "I think so." She grabbed Worth by the shoulder and pulled him to her. "First, you ain't got no damn shirt, and that's gonna be noticed. Second, where the hell is Riley?"

Worth looked at William. "Questions. Riley. Now her. Always questions."

"You're telling me, bud." William walked to the other side of Worth so that the drunks and guards wouldn't see a man standing shirtless on the street. "But, we need to get out of here and get to Riley."

"Worth know. Worth know." He rolled his eyes as if nothing could be more obvious.

"Well, where is she?" Lucie hissed.

Worth's eyes narrowed as he swayed on his feet. "Hmmmm..."

"Oh you bastard," Lucie said, really growing angry. If she'd had a pan from her restaurant, she would have clocked him upside the head with it right then and there.

Worth smiled. "Kidding. Kidding. She hiding. Worth say he find you, and now he did. He bring you to her. Come."

The bald man turned without another word and started walking down the street. He didn't have a care in the world, shirt or no shirt. Ten steps in he started singing.

"I missed the bastard," William said.

"Yeah. I missed him like I miss a toothache. Come on before the drunk starts runnin'," Lucie responded.

The two followed the singing bald man down the street.

"You tired?" Riley asked.

Eric was bent over, his hands on his knees, panting.

"If it hadn't been for that ladder I wouldn't have had a chance in hell," he responded.

Riley was realizing how much better she was with a sword than the young man. He'd done well on the ladder when they faced each other before, but that's because he was used to such things. On the ground, where she held the experience, he was good, but she was better.

She slapped the back of his leg with the flat of her sword. "Can't get tired so soon. Have to work on your lungs. Up. *Again.*"

Eric straightened and assumed a defensive posture.

"Defense is rarely what you want," she told him.

"You're a better opponent. I can't attack you," he responded.

Riley smiled. "Defense is waiting to die. That's all. Offense is a warrior's way."

"Is that why you made us come here before you're ready?" He wasn't grinning.

Riley's smile died too. "Maybe. I go forward, I don't wait. I've learned what I think I need to learn to face Rendal, and that's the only reason I'm learning magic. Despite what the Chosen say, I'm not their savior. I'm *Mason's* savior, and when that is finished, I'm going home. No more magic."

Thomas stood at the far side of the basement watching the two practice. He said nothing as she spoke.

"Now, is that the posture you want?"

Eric nodded.

"Stubborn." Riley flashed another grin. "Fine."

She started forward, her feet dancing left and right, not committing to any one path.

Her sword clashed down. Eric's met it, the resulting clang echoing in the small space.

She spun.

Eric met her.

She spun again, feigning. Eric bit, his sword stretching out to meet hers...that was no longer there.

Riley brought her sword down on Eric's neck, stopping it exactly when steel touched flesh. "You're dead, dear."

He panted as he chuckled and bent over again, his hands on his knees.

"How did I beat you?" she asked.

"You're too fast. I can't keep up."

Riley shook her head. "No matter how fast I am, my muscles will never be as strong as most men's, so that's not the case. Try again. How did I beat you?"

He shook his head, looking at his feet. "I don't know."

"You'll keep losing until you do," she answered.

"I'll never be able to beat you."

Riley slapped his ass with the flat of her sword. "Not until you figure out why I'm winning. Enough for tonight. Get cleaned up and go to bed."

Eric nodded and started up the basement stairs.

Riley turned to Thomas, who was still standing in the

corner. "The queen wasn't lying about knowing people. I'm grateful to you for getting us this place to stay."

"My Savior, this is the least we can do. Every single one of us would lay down our lives for you if you ask."

Riley wanted to shake her head but smiled instead. It would be disrespectful to show exasperation. No matter how hard she tried, Thomas believed she was the one to...well, to lead the world into the future.

"Anyway," Riley responded. "Thanks."

Alexandra had been playing coy. The Chosen were actually extremely wealthy, as this house showed, or they still had family that were, at least.

Not all of the Chosen's lineage believed what Alexandra and those who lived underground did. Many thought they were loons, but family was family, apparently.

Thomas had shown up at this house, and while the proprietor wasn't *happy* to see him, the man didn't turn them away, either.

They were given bedrooms, food, and a place to practice sword work down here.

Riley looked up, the fear coming back to her.

"The owner isn't going to report us, right? He's not going to tell anyone we're here?"

Thomas smiled. "No, my Savior. While Bruce may not agree with our beliefs, he's Alexandra's uncle. He's not going to do anything to hurt her or me."

She nodded.

Riley trusted this man as much as she did Worth.

Worth. Where the hell was he?

It'd been hours. The night was turning into morning now, yet she'd seen no sign of the tent man.

"You're worried, my Savior?" Thomas asked.

She raised her eyebrows. "Studying me that hard? I remember that when I first showed up to your home, you weren't too impressed."

Thomas dropped his eyes to the floor. "I will apologize forever for the way I acted. It's just... We've had so many imposters over the years. So many people who tried to fool us. It was tough to believe you were the one."

Riley smiled wide. "I'm joking, Thomas. No worries. I'm just thinking about Worth, and whether he went and got stinking drunk instead of looking for William and the others."

"You trust him? Worth?" Thomas asked.

"Oh, yeah. He drinks a lot, but he's shown his dedication more times than I can count."

Thomas looked a bit confused. "But you think he might be getting drunk instead of doing what you told him?"

"Worth likes his wine," Riley told him. "But no. I think he's out there looking for them—"

A loud crash echoed down the stairs, Riley's head immediately turning that way.

"Worth home!"

Riley looked at Thomas. "Oh, no. I'm sorry."

"*RILEY!*" William's voice boomed down the stairs.

Riley's eyes widened, but she didn't waste any time. She flew up the stairs. She was no longer thinking about Thomas or Worth, only the voice screaming for her.

"*RILEY, YOU LAZY GOOD FER NOTHING, WHERE ARE YOU? I BET YOU'RE ASLEEP!*"

She hit the last stair, then turned down the hall.

William stood in it, as big as ever.

There were healing burns on his arms and cheek, but—

"Glad you could fuckin' make it." His deep voice easily crossed the space between them. "We've actually been workin' here in these parts."

Riley ran down the hall, ignoring his wisecracks.

She wrapped her arms around William, embracing him.

"Always with the emotions. No one around here wants to hug ya, girl." Even as he said the words, his arms wrapped around Riley.

Worth stumbled into the hallway behind William, Lucie following him.

"This one!" Worth shouted. "Questions! Questions! Never stop."

Riley pulled away, looking at Worth. "Oh, dear. He's shit-faced. Tell me you to didn't *encourage* this."

"Encourage?" Lucie asked. "Hardly, girl. We found him like this. You're the one who was supposed to be watchin' him. Or he you. Both of you're s'posed to be watching the other, and it seems like you're the one who failed."

Riley moved past William and down the hall to Lucie. "I missed you." She embraced the older woman.

"Missed you too, girl. Glad you made it back."

"Who the hell is that?" William grumbled as Thomas found his way to the top stair.

"Him? That's Thomas," Riley said as she pulled away from Lucie. "He's from underground."

"The underground people?" William asked.

"The *Chosen*," Thomas corrected from the other end of the hall.

William looked at Riley. "Oh he's a proper one, ain't he?

I'll have to break him of it. What the hell you bring him for?"

"For one, he helped us *get* here," Riley told William. "Two, he also is the reason we're in this house. Given the way you smell, William, you might want to walk down there and ask Thomas if you can stay."

Thomas shook his head. "No. He can go back to where he came from."

William turned, his face angry. "Who the hell you think you're talkin' to?"

"Calm down, dummy," Lucie instructed.

"My Savior is right. You smell far too ripe to stay here with us," Thomas said without the slightest smirk.

William's anger fled from his face, his eyebrows raising...and raising...

He slowly turned and looked at Riley. "What... What did he say?"

Riley didn't know whether to laugh or run from embarrassment. So instead, she said nothing.

Looking back at Thomas, William asked, "What did you call her?"

"My Savior."

William groaned loudly, falling back against the wall as if struck by some large object. "Ya gotta be fuckin' *kiddin'* me." He brought a hand to his brow, rubbing it briskly. "She's got a fuckin' cult. Riley's got a fuckin' *cult.*"

Riley laughed. "See? You better start treating me nicer, William, or you might just end up *missing.*"

CHAPTER FIVE

Brighten only had the slightest clue who Riley Trident was, and he had no idea that she'd shown up on the night he and Erin were committing suicide.

That was how *he* thought of it, anyway.

Erin just seemed to think it was a damned adventure.

"You ready?" she'd asked before they left Connor's.

"No." Brighten had shaken his head.

Erin had winked at him. "Life's too short to be so scared. Let's live a little, aye?"

Brighten could see that William was falling for her. She was beautiful; that stood out perhaps before anything else. Yet, Brighten really *liked* her too. He couldn't help but like her, and he didn't think anyone else could either.

She was contagious—her energy and her *good-naturedness*.

The magic class had ended about ten minutes ago, and Brighten was once again exhausted. He was concentrating harder than he ever had before; *much* harder than he did when they were stealing on the streets.

Rendal, the headmaster or dark mage, taught that there was only *one* magic, but for ease of understanding, people often divided them up.

The magic Brighten felt drawn to was something Rendal called Psychic magic, although he said other people called it different things.

It was the easiest for Brighten, and he supposed that was because he'd had a predilection for it for years. It was one of the reasons he and Kris made such good thieves.

Other people in the class took to other magics, and so far, no one had noticed Brighten—or at least not because of anything out of the ordinary.

Other mages were in the class, helping teach. Brighten always made sure he worked with one of them and never Rendal.

Never Rendal.

The man was terrifying.

The whole thing took a lot of concentration, and Brighten was once again exhausted, but he couldn't go back to Connor's. Instead, he was still inside the castle's walls, waiting for Erin to finish her training.

He had a cigarette in his hand and was leaning against a tree. He puffed it occasionally but didn't breathe anything into his lungs. Blending in had always been a necessity for Brighten, so he'd learned ways to look older. Smoking was one of them.

Another ten minutes passed with him slowly letting the cigarette burn down. He'd almost decided that he was going to kill Kris when he saw her next. He didn't *look* scared, but inside he was terrified.

Finally, the damned military let out from their drills.

Brighten had seen them over the past few days, and the people exiting the training facility were definitely evolving.

Growing stronger.

More disciplined.

And scarier.

They left in lines now, no longer mobs of people simply walking across the castle's yards.

Brighten remained where he was, his sharp eyes searching for Erin.

She saw him and his burning cigarette almost at the same time.

She didn't wave or give any other indication, only slightly turned away from the line she was in and crossed the dark courtyard.

"How ya feeling?" she asked when she reached him.

"Like my anxiety is eating me alive. We don't have to do this," he told her. "We can go back to the group and just say we couldn't get to it."

Erin smiled at him, a motherly smile. "You're scared, and I understand that, but that has never stopped you before, Brighten. You grew up on the fucking streets. You steal for your meals on a daily basis. You can be scared, but you're *not* weak."

Brighten dropped his eyes, unable to hold Erin's strong gaze.

"You hear me?" she asked. "You're strong—you and Kris both. I knew it from the moment I laid eyes on the both of you."

He nodded. She was right. Brighten *was* always scared, but he'd been through things other kids his age couldn't imagine. He'd been through them and come out on the other side.

"Come on," he said. "Let's go get ourselves killed."

He flicked the cigarette away, and the two walked into the darkness.

"I think of them as the catacombs," Brighten whispered as they moved away from the large crowd of soldiers.

"Why? Are there dead bodies in the tunnels?"

Brighten shrugged. "I don't know. Just seems fitting. Scarier, too."

"Oh, goodness. Eric and I have some things to teach you," she responded, shaking her head.

Another minute or so passed while they walked in silence. Brighten was impressed with Erin's ability to not make any noise, as if she'd been a thief her whole life.

"Stop." Erin put her arm out in front of Brighten's chest. "You don't hear them? The guards?"

Brighten smiled. She moved quietly, but she didn't have his senses. "I heard them thirty feet ago."

"Then why are you still walking *toward* them?" Erin asked.

"What the hell ya think I'm doing every night, Erin? I'm not goin' to that magic class to twiddle my thumbs. I'm learnin'."

Erin still didn't take her arm away from his chest. She was staring forward and he could sense her muscles tightening, readying for a fight. She wouldn't run and Brighten respected her for that.

Yet, they didn't have to fight anyone, or at least not these two guards up ahead.

"Just *trust* me, okay?" he whispered.

She looked down at him, judging whether to believe. She finally nodded and dropped her hand. Good thing for Brighten, because if she didn't want him moving, he wasn't gonna be able to. The woman was lethal.

They kept walking, rounding a darkened corner, and then they were in front of the two guards.

There was a lantern on a stone wall behind them, and both were seated in chairs and chatting.

The two looked up at the sight of Brighten and Erin.

"You fuckin' lost?" the one on the left asked.

"Gotta be," the other agreed, standing up and placing his hand on his sword. "If you're in that damned magic school or one of the newbs training for the military, you're way outta line coming here. Skedaddle back to where you came from."

"How about—" Erin started to say something but Brighten jabbed her with his elbow.

He didn't look away from the guards.

"What were ya about to say, ya tramp?" the first guard asked, stepping forward. "Every fuckin' streetwalker thinks she's special now 'cause they can all join the army. Ya need to understand that inside *this* place, this castle—we rule, so think for another second before those dumbass words drop out of your mouth, you understand?"

Brighten smiled. He hadn't planned on being a dick to these guys, but he didn't like how they were talking to Erin one bit.

His eyes turned red.

"Hey!" the first guard shouted.

"You can't do that without permiss—"

Shh, Brighten said with his mind. *No need to be so loud.*

109

The two men still looked angry, but they'd both stopped speaking.

"What are you doing to them?" Erin asked.

"Just talking," he responded.

Rendal had been teaching them that Psychic Magic could influence people. It could make them think things they might not otherwise. It could even make them forget things, or *do* things. It all depended on the magic user's strength and the subject's weakness.

These two were weak, thank the Father and Mother.

We're not really here, Brighten told them. *You're not seeing us right now.*

He felt their minds trying to resist, so Brighten focused harder, his mind *bending* theirs.

You both feel bad, though, because earlier you called a nice lady a tramp, Brighten instructed. *You feel guilty. And to prove it, both of you are going to cluck like chickens for the next two hours.*

He thought two hours might be beyond his ability, that their minds would snap back before then, but that was okay.

The man on the left started walking in a circle, his leg movements overly pronounced like that of a bird. His head moved backward and forward with each step, looking exactly like a chicken.

"BAWK! BAWK!" the second guard said.

"What the fuck are they doing, Brighten?" Erin asked, real concern in her voice.

Brighten smiled, the flames in his eyes dying away. "They feel guilty for calling you a tramp, so now they're going to cluck like chickens for a while."

"BAWK!" the first one yapped, still walking in a circle, his head pecking forward.

"Come on, let's keep moving," Brighten told her. "I don't know how long it'll hold."

She laughed. "That's ridiculous. You learned that in school?"

"Oh, yeah." Brighten started walking down the path, leaving the lantern's light and returning to the darkness. "We're learning a lot up there. That's why I'm so damned tired all the time."

Erin was still laughing as she jogged to catch up. "That's amazing. They think they're chickens?"

"No, not quite," Brighten tried to explain. "I'm not completely sure. I mean, I just started learnin' this stuff. They feel like they did something wrong, so that's their penance. I took a sort of fatherly tone with them? That might be the best way to explain it."

"Will they remember us?" she asked.

"Nah, or at least not enough to talk about it. I'm not strong enough to erase minds, but I think I kind of moved the memory around so that they won't ever focus on it."

"Amazing," Erin whispered. "So, you don't really need me here, right? Like, I could leave? Because you can just basically walk through an army by yourself."

"Hell, no!" Brighten turned around, real fear on his face.

"I'm just kidding." Erin reached out and touched the boy's shoulder. "I'm not going anywhere. But, if you wanted, you really could go far into the 'catacombs.' What you did back there was amazing."

"Only with two people, and really close up. I don't

know how far I can push it." He started walking again, glad Erin wasn't ditching him.

The catacombs could only be reached from *inside* the castle, but Brighten navigated the route. He didn't think Rendal understood the potential trouble he was creating for himself, training an entire generation in magic usage.

Brighten used the new psychic abilities to move through the hallways of the castle without being detected. He understood when people were coming, and even what they were focusing on.

"We almost there?" Erin whispered after a group of sentries passed, completely oblivious to their existence.

"You're as impatient as Kris," Brighten insisted. "We can't just run down the halls. We have to be careful."

Erin smirked. "I know, I know. I'm just ready to see what this bastard is creating."

The two scurried through the castle until they reached a final hallway.

"As far as I know, it's down there," Brighten whispered.

"As far as you *know*?" Erin asked.

He shrugged. "Hey, you people are the ones who told me we had to go. This is where Kris and I think it is, but how in the hell are we supposed to *know* if we ain't never been down there?"

"You hear them?" Erin asked, moving past her first question.

"Of course," Brighten answered. "I think there's six of 'em." He was talking about the guards. The corridor before them was lit by lanterns every ten feet or so on either side.

"You can use your magic to defeat that many?" Erin asked.

"No way," Brighten told her. "I'm exhausted, and those two back there pushed me beyond my limits. We need to leave. Go back to Connor's."

Erin smiled and stepped into the poorly lit hallway. She raised her hands above her head, interlacing her fingers together, and *stretched*. Her knuckles and joints popped.

"Feels good," she whispered.

"What the fuck are you doing?" Brighten barely held his voice to a whisper.

Erin raised one of her legs, pulling her foot to her ass and stretching her quad. "Loosening up. You're about to see some pretty sweet action, Brighten. Enjoy it."

She looked over her shoulder and gave him a wink before turning back to the hall.

"Hey, boys. I'm about to come in there and beat your asses. You ready?"

Brighten's stomach rose into his throat and his whole body went cold.

"Who the fuck is down there?" someone hollered from the circular room at the end. Brighten couldn't see into it.

"Come and find out." Erin's voice echoed off the ceiling.

A man's face appeared at the opposite end. "You ain't supposed to be here."

The other men walked up behind him, all looking at the gorgeous redhead in the ancient hallway.

"This is *exactly* where I'm supposed to be," Erin told them. "Because you folks are guarding something, and I plan on finding out what."

"Little lady, take your pretty ass out of here right now. If you don't listen to me, my men and I here are gonna beat you so bad you're not going to be able to open your eyes for two weeks." The man seemed slightly amused at this strange turn of events.

"This 'little lady' is going to break a lot of bones when you finally quit being such dickweeds. Isn't your job to protect something back there? Why ain't ya doing it?"

She took a step forward.

"Fuck it, boss. Let's get her," another guard responded.

They came forward then, although they couldn't walk more than two deep due to the hallway's width.

Brighten knew immediately that was exactly what Erin wanted.

The first two had short swords, little more than daggers.

"You going to make us cut you, or you going to go ahead and lay down face-first on the floor?" the man on the left asked. "Either way is fine with me."

"I wonder if you wield them swords better than the short dicks in between your legs," Erin shot back.

Well, that's one way to answer, Brighten thought. His heart was beating double-time, and he wanted to run from this place without ever looking back.

He knew he couldn't, though. He had to watch what happened here.

The first two soldiers awkwardly moved toward Erin, and when they arrived, they didn't seem to know exactly how to attack her. The quarters were too tight.

Erin had no such problem. One of them swung their sword while the other reached out to grab her shoulder.

She simply moved back, the sword driving into the other soldier's arm.

A loud scream, and a spurt of blood. Erin ignored both,

kicking high—first left, then right. The two dropped to the floor, unconscious.

The second two were right there waiting, both realizing that they were in real danger. The one on the left stepped forward, wielding a black club. He swung, but Erin dropped to a knee and shot her fist out.

She nailed him right in the groin. He let out a horrible groan, the club falling to the floor and his hands going to his balls.

Erin rose to her feet, swinging her knee as she did. She caught the soldier in his nose, cracking it and knocking him out at the same time.

The second one lunged, which was a horrible mistake. Erin sliced an uppercut through the air, landing it on the man's chin. Brighten saw his eyes roll back into his head before he fell on top of his partner.

Two left.

Neither of them wanted a thing to do with the redheaded phantom who had just dropped two-thirds of their party.

They looked at each other, both clearly deciding they'd be safer back where they'd come from.

They turned to run.

"Oh, come on, little dicks! The party's just getting started!"

Erin rushed down the hallway, making no noise as she caught up with the guards.

She could have hurt them any way she wanted, but Brighten saw the kindness in what she did—although the guards probably didn't.

She clacked their heads together *hard*.

A *thud* echoed through the hallway, and two more bodies fell to the ground.

Erin turned and looked at Brighten. "Whatcha waitin' on, buttercup?"

His eyes were wide. He'd never seen anything like that in his life.

None of those on the floor were moving. Some might actually be *dying*, yet she stood completely untouched.

"What *are* you?" he asked.

"A pirate...or a former pirate." She winked. "Come on, there's more to do."

Brighten came down the hall toward her, stepping over the fallen guards. "What if this isn't the right place?"

"Then why are there so many guards for this small part of the castle? Six people to sit here at the end of this little hallway, for what? There's nothing else on this side of the castle." Erin shook her head as they exited the hall. "Nope, you were right. This is the 'catacombs,' and this is where they're hiding those weapons."

They entered a circular room made of brick. Six chairs indicated where the soldiers had been, as well as cards on the floor.

"They're guarding this, but clearly they don't feel there is any threat. They were playing damned card games." Erin pointed at the floor. "Still, despite there being no threats, someone told them to come sit here."

She looked at Brighten with a mischievous grin.

"They're hiding something, baby boy."

He rolled his eyes. "I'm not a baby. Come on."

A wooden door with a circular handle interrupted the brick wall. He reached for it.

"Oh, there's the bravery we need!" Erin said gleefully.

Brighten shook his head. "Nope. There's no one on the other side. I'd know. We're safe for a little while, at least."

Brighten's stomach was actually coiling into knots, but he wasn't going to tell Erin that—especially not after watching her kick six grown men's asses.

He pulled on the door, and it groaned beneath the force, then slowly opened.

Another hallway looked back at him. The air inside smelled stale.

It was obviously slanted downward, descending to the depths of the castle.

"How far do you think it goes?" Erin asked.

"How the hell do I know? Kris is the one who found this place." Brighten shook his head. "I need to stop hanging out with her. She's always getting me into shit I don't want."

"That means you got a good woman, Brighten. You want one who keeps you on your toes." Erin winked at him, then walked past. "Try to keep up, baby boy."

"I'm not a baby!" he whispered harshly, but Erin was already moving quickly away from him.

He shook his head and followed her into the tunnel's depths.

"Have you found her?" Rendal asked with his eyes closed.

Harold had just walked into the tower's top floor, and he didn't like the stress he saw on Rendal's face.

"No, sir. We're still looking," he answered his master.

Rendal opened his eyes. "That's *not* good enough."

"I know," Harold answered.

"If you fucking *know*, why don't you have her?"

"I'm doing the best I can, sir. We will find her."

Rendal stood up, his head whipping toward Mason, who stood on the opposite side of the room. He was looking out a window at the kingdom. It was still dark, and a light rain had been falling for hours.

"They're fucking hiding her from me," Rendal cursed at Mason. "And they're doing it on *purpose*."

"Having trouble, master mage?" Mason asked without turning around.

"You're going to be having real trouble real soon if you don't watch your tongue," Rendal spat back.

Mason turned around and leaned against the window. "You know what I think you need, Rendal? A wife. A wife and maybe a kid or two might help you calm down. I'm starting to worry about your stress level."

Mason was grinning.

Harold wasn't sure exactly what would happen next. He hadn't seen Rendal this pissed since... Well, maybe since ever. The mage had been able to tell when Riley arrived in Sidnie, but now he'd lost her.

He just kept saying, "They're hiding her from me."

Mason might not care if Rendal tossed him off the tower, but Harold wanted to continue living. He'd been given his instructions: find her.

So, that was what he was trying to do.

Rendal's face was growing red. Mason should have known to keep his mouth shut, but the man apparently wanted to push Rendal.

"Tell me, grand mage," the Assistant Prefect continued, "why are you so upset right now? What about her returning this time has you in such a hissy?"

Rendal swallowed but said nothing.

"I know, I know. You haven't asked me, Rendal, but if you want my opinion, I think you're upset because you're scared." Mason shrugged. "Which makes sense. Riley *is* a badass. And if she's learned magic now? Whew!"

Mason sighed.

"She's not someone *I'd* want to fuck with, ya know what I mean?"

Rendal walked across the room. A vein was bulging in his neck. "You know you're only making your death more painful, right? With each little smartass remark, you're ensuring that when I kill you, I'm going to make it that much *worse?*"

Mason said nothing but kept wearing that grin.

Rendal turned around, bringing his attention back to Harold—which Harold didn't want.

"Where have you searched?"

"Sir, we started in the poorer areas of town," Harold answered. "We're moving through the shanties and shelters since that's where it'd be easiest to find help. The upper-class citizens aren't going to risk bringing in strangers right now. They have too much to lose."

"I don't give a damn about class, Harold. Go through the rich and the poor. How many fucking guards are we using?" The vein in Rendal's neck looked like it might explode.

"Half, sir. The other half have training, regular duties, and—"

"Pull 'em off," Rendal snapped. "All of them. Take as many as you need."

Harold blinked. "Sir, the rest of your plans will *halt*."

"You damned idiot!" Rendal screamed. "Find a way to keep them going! Should I replace you with Belarus?"

"No, sir. I'll make sure it happens."

Rendal looked away, staring at the light drizzle falling on the balcony. He walked toward a window on the other side of the room, Harold relishing the newfound silence.

"I can't find her," Rendal whispered. Harold didn't know if Rendal was talking to him or simply thinking aloud. "Those damned fool friends of hers are hiding her. They're blocking me from seeing. And someone *inside* this kingdom is hiding her, too. Someone is going against my will."

Harold didn't want to speak, but it was his duty. "Sir, she could be hiding with no one's help. Sidnie is a huge place. There are a lot of buildings she could stow away in as long as she kept moving."

Rendal shook his head. He didn't show anger, though, and Harold almost pissed himself in relief. "No, someone's hiding her. And that's okay."

Rendal turned around, his rage completely disappearing. "That's okay, then. If they want to keep her from me, I'll just make the price too high."

"What do you mean?" Mason asked from the other side of the room.

Rendal turned his grin on Mason. "The boy wonder doesn't seem so arrogant now. A bit worried, yes?"

Everyone in the room is worried, Harold thought.

Rendal looked positively mad.

"The price for holding the Right Hand just rose to death." Rendal looked at Harold. "Go forth and make it so, my dear Harold."

"Yes, sir." Harold turned and walked from the tower. He closed the door after him and remained on the top step.

He let his heart return to a normal pattern, staring at the steps below him.

Harold didn't give a damn about killing the citizens of the stupid kingdom. He just didn't want to get himself killed in the process, and Rendal hadn't looked exactly *stable.*

The head guard walked down the steps.

He went straight to Belarus's room in the castle.

He didn't knock, simply burst inside.

Belarus's bed was in the center of the room. Two women popped up from beneath the covers, one on either side of Belarus.

"What the fuck?" Belarus said groggily, pulling himself from his slumber and climbing out from beneath the blankets.

"What was that, Belarus? I don't think I heard you correctly," Harold asked, still standing in the open doorway.

Belarus's eyes grew to the size of eggs. "Sorry, boss. Sorry. I didn't know it was you. Sorry."

He was rambling, and Harold didn't have time for it. He closed the door and lit a lantern to his right.

"Who the hell is that?" one of the whores asked, clearly not pleased about having been woken.

Harold's eyebrows raised. "Who am *I*?"

"You gonna get rid of him?" the other whore asked.

Belarus' eyes were still huge. He reached over and smacked the woman on his left, then shoved the one on his right off the bed. She shrieked as her bare ass hit the floor.

"Get outta here, both of ya!" Belarus stepped from the bed as he shouted, dragging the other woman with him. He threw her toward the door.

She turned around, staring at Belarus. "That wasn't worth the money or the sleep, with your little bitty dick!"

"Oh, hush it, whore. Just get outta here."

Harold watched with a slight smile as the women made their way from the room, shouting obscenities about the size of Belarus's genitals.

Finally, the door was closed and the two were alone.

"Have a good night last night, Belarus?" Harold asked.

"Sorry, boss. I ain't expect ya to just show up like that. I mean, you're more than welcome to. Can come and go as you please, that's the way I look at it."

Harold waved the groveling away. "Just hush. We've got things to discuss."

"More?" Belarus asked.

The man's going to open his mouth like that in front of Rendal one day, Harold thought, *and the mage is going to take his whole head off for his tongue's offense.*

"Yes, more. That okay with you?"

"'Course, boss. 'Course it's okay. We just... Well, ya know, we got a lot goin' on already, wouldn't ya say?" Belarus asked.

The man had no damned filter. He was dumber than a bag of nails, and Harold was *cursed* with him.

"It doesn't matter. Plans are changing, Belarus, and once again, I'd advise you to keep your fucking trap shut unless you feel like your life has been too long and you're ready to step away from it. You understand what I'm telling you, Belarus?"

The guard swallowed, nodding hard. "Yeah, boss. I got it. I understand."

"Good." Harold moved across the room and looked at the bed. He thought about sitting on it for about half a second, then chose a chair at a small desk. "Sit down, Belarus."

He hustled to the bed and sat as quickly as a puppy expecting a treat.

"You remember Riley, right? The woman who broke your arm?"

"I remember the bitch," Belarus spat. "If I see her again, I'm gonna break more than her fuckin' arm."

Harold sighed. He wanted to throat-punch the man, but it would do no good. "Perhaps you'll get your chance. She's here."

"In Sidnie?" Belarus asked.

"No, in this room, you damned fool. Yes, *Sidnie.* The mage believes people are hiding her. He wants us to kill anyone we think knows something."

A slow smile spread across Belarus's face as he took in what Harold was saying. "We're gonna hurt people?"

"Yes, we're going to hurt people."

"How?" Belarus asked.

"That's what we have to work out, *Belarus.*" Harold's

patience was growing thin. Perhaps he should just kill Belarus and get another second-in-command.

He couldn't yet, though. There was too much to be done.

Harold kept talking. "The goal here is to hurt people and put fear into the rest. We want people more scared of us than they are of giving up those people."

Belarus nodded. This was simple. This was something he *got*. Hurt folks and spread that message around.

"I'll do it, boss. When do you want me to get started?"

"Well, Belarus," Harold said, "you ever heard a saying about there being no time like the present?"

"Naw, boss," Belarus answered. "Never heard that."

Harold stared in silence at the idiot across from him. Belarus looked like he was waiting for Harold to say something else.

Harold spoke slowly. "That saying means you should get started *now*. Right *fucking* now."

Understanding spread over Belarus's face. "Yes, boss. Yes. Right now. I'll get started."

"Right now?" Harold asked.

Belarus nodded. "Right now."

"Then why the fuck are you still sitting on the bed?"

Belarus jumped up, rushing to put clothes on. Harold closed his eyes and shook his head. If that Riley bitch saw Belarus, he was as good as dead.

Which was fine with Harold. A lot of people in Sidnie were about to die, so what was one more?

CHAPTER SIX

"We're getting close to people," Brighten whispered. "I can feel someone up ahead."

The tunnel had wound farther down for the past half-hour. They hadn't seen anyone since closing the door behind them.

Yet now Brighten brought them to a halt.

"How far?" Erin asked.

"I don't know. This stuff is new to me," he answered.

"Well, come on. We'll figure it out." Erin took the lead, moving through the hallway, albeit slower.

It circled to the right.

Both Erin and Brighten stopped.

The hallway had felt endless to Brighten, nothing like the catacombs he'd built up in his mind.

"Wow!" Erin whispered.

Brighten moved forward, stepping up next to Erin and looking at the room before him. It was massive, so large he could hardly understand how it existed down here. It was all brick, with round columns stretching from floor to ceiling throughout. Around the walls were enclaves that looked like open workrooms, at least right now.

"You felt some people, eh?" Erin whispered again.

Brighten was too enraptured to be frightened, although he should have been.

People swarmed the room. Carrying objects, standing over wooden tables with small tools in their hands, testing...

"What the fuck are those?" Brighten said, pointing to the right side of the room.

Three men stood in a wide circle. They each had on red necklaces, and their eyes were red too. Brighten didn't care about the necklaces or the red eyes; they were clearly practicing magic. Instead, he was staring at the *inside* of the circle.

Three orbs hung in the middle. They were black with green lines running around them.

"Start," a man said.

Brighten hadn't seen him before. He was shorter and not wearing a necklace, and his eyes were a normal brown.

The other three men didn't look at him, just stared forward, their faces lax.

Each orb shot to one of the men, hanging directly in front of his face.

"Go," the short man said.

The orbs started to *fly*. They remained inside the circle but were rushing around the inside edge of it one after the other, picking up speed. Round and round, the black and green becoming blurs.

"Good," the short man commented, nodding. "This is good. This is what we want."

"Why are they doing that?" Brighten asked, not expecting an answer.

Erin shook her head.

The short man walked away from the men, although they didn't move. Their faces didn't change one bit.

Brighten figured the person he should be watching was the short man; he seemed to be in charge.

He moved across the floor, not noticing anything or anyone, completely lost in his own head. He looked to be talking to himself beneath his breath.

He walked closer to Brighten and Erin. So far no one had noticed them. The room was simply too busy and big to see the quiet new entrants.

The short man stopped and Brighten saw what he'd missed: three cages. The short man now stood in front of them, looking at the occupants.

"Please," one of the men in the cages pleaded. "Please let us go. We won't say anything. We won't tell anyone what's happening down here."

Brighten half believed the guy because he couldn't figure out what the hell was happening down here himself.

The short man didn't respond. He simply stepped away, backing up against the wall.

"*GO!*" he shouted, turning his head to the three people wearing necklaces.

"What the hell is happening?" Erin whispered harshly.

Brighten had no idea. This was all too weird. His eyes flashed to the three lax-faced men, none of whom moved.

However, the black orbs immediately stopped racing around in their circle. They bolted through an opening between the three men, rushing across the room. They moved faster than any horse or bird Brighten had ever seen. Faster than anything he could imagine.

His eyes caught the intricacies of their movement. They were rolling as they flew, and a line of holes opened up across the surface.

Brighten's eyes widened. He was completely confused but unable to look away.

He heard the sound of something popping, then there were screams from the cages. His eyes flew to them. The people inside were bleeding, and—

Pop. Pop. Pop.

The sounds were like tiny air pockets bursting, and then the people in the cages were bleeding from *more* holes.

Their faces. Their sides.

Pop. Pop. Pop.

The three dropped to the floor, dying if not dead.

Brighten looked at the orbs.

They hung in the air five feet from the cages.

The holes perforating their surfaces were still there, and tiny metal balls rested just inside.

Brighten glanced at the dead.

"That's not possible," he whispered, dread filling him.

"You saw it," Erin answered. "I did, too. It's possible."

Brighten swallowed. He didn't understand anything of what he had just seen, or least not *how* it had happened. He was smart enough to understand *what* had happened, though.

The men at the end, those wearing red necklaces, just used magic to race those orbs across the room. The orbs then shot out those tiny metal balls.

And the people in the cages? They died from the injuries the balls caused.

The short man was squatting, looking at the people in the cages. Studying them.

"Come on," Erin said. "That's just one experiment. There are more, I'm sure. We need to see them."

"What the hell are you talkin' about, Erin? I'm not going anywhere but right back out that tunnel to Kris. Then I'm tellin' her we're done here. We're done with you, William, Lucie, and everyone else. That right there—that just eliminated the need for archers. It eliminated the need for soldiers because someone can control those orbs from *anywhere*. Those orbs just changed warfare."

He didn't look at Erin as he spoke. He stared at the three people in the cages, all of them dead now.

The smack upside his head pulled his attention from them.

Erin was looking down at him, the motherly visage from earlier gone. No awe at his psychic abilities.

A redheaded fury stood in front of him. "Listen here, runt. Those people you just said you're done with? Those are my friends, and they're the only ones willing to stop that psychopath down there from using those orbs on everyone in this kingdom. You want to turn around and go, be my fucking guest. But I promise that when I finish here, I'm going to come find you for being such a bitch."

"I-I-I..." Brighten tried to stutter something out but couldn't manage to find the words.

"*I* know you're scared, but there's duty involved here, and we're not going to shirk it out of fear. Get your shit together and let's keep looking. We haven't been noticed yet, and I think there's a good chance we can see a lot more before we are. I need you to help keep us from being seen with your magic. There's more to find out, and we're gonna do it. Okay?"

Brighten wanted to nod. He wanted to say yes. He wanted to be brave, but he couldn't find the strength. He couldn't make himself talk.

Erin smiled, the fury fading.

"It's okay. I don't need an answer, but if you quit acting like a bitch and come with me, I'll brag all about it to Kris and William. They won't be able to say shit for at least a week."

That broke through his paralysis—the thought of him being able to lord this over Kris.

He grinned. "You promise you'll tell them?"

"Hell yeah, I will," Erin answered. "You in?"

He laughed. "I'd do anything to be able to make fun of Kris without her having any ammo to come back at me with."

"Then let's turn you into a legend, shall we?"

Daybreak came, but Riley didn't wake up as the light shone through her window. Perhaps it was the exhaustion of travel, or maybe it was only that she felt her friends were safe.

The knock on the door brought her from her slumber.

She sat up quickly in her bed, though her mind wasn't in attack mode.

"Come in," she said. She was still wearing her clothes from the previous evening.

Thomas walked into the room and closed the door behind him. "I apologize, my Savior. I didn't want to wake you, but I'm not sure this can be avoided."

"Thomas! Stop with the savior stuff!" Riley grumbled good-naturedly.

"I'm sorry." He nodded, looking down. "I'll work harder at it."

She sighed and stood up. "It's okay. It's just awkward for me. I'm nobody's savior." Riley turned and started making her bed.

"There's trouble, my—Riley."

"When is there not?" Riley groaned. She didn't stop making her bed as she asked, "What is it?"

"Bruce came to me early this morning. The kingdom is looking for you."

That caught Riley's attention. She turned around. "What do you mean?"

"This mage, Rendal—he knows you're here," Thomas explained. "And apparently he's willing to do anything to find you."

"Are you trying to give me a heart attack, Thomas? Tell me what the hell is going on." Riley smirked. The man could be long-winded when he had information he didn't want to give her.

"They're searching houses, the kingdom's guards. Even the military. They're going through rich and poor alike, and they're ripping places apart."

Riley felt somewhat confused. "That makes no sense. No one in this kingdom knows I exist besides Rendal. I understand that he might know I'm here, but what's going through every single house going to do? Unless he finds *this* one, he won't find me."

"Yes." Thomas sighed. "That's one way to look at it, but if I may be so bold, I don't think it's the correct way."

"Thomas! Be bold, man! What the hell is going on out there?" Riley wanted to laugh *and* throttle the man. When he'd first met her, he had been nothing but rude, but now he could hardly bear to give her bad news.

"I spoke to Lucie earlier this morning. She is much better than that oaf William." Thomas shook his head at the mention of the Right Hand's name. "She says it's only partially about finding you. It's also about—"

"Showing me that if I don't come forward, he's going to hurt people." Riley stopped talking as the truth came to her. The depravity of it, something she hadn't been able to even imagine moments before.

Thomas nodded in agreement. "Yes. He's going to kill people until they start talking, and then they're going to say anything. They'll start ratting out neighbors and friends who have nothing to do with this to keep themselves safe."

Riley looked at Thomas, her face hard. "Has there been an official proclamation?"

"Yes," Thomas answered. "Anyone housing the spies will be considered enemies of the state."

"Where is everybody else?"

"Everyone is downstairs except for the Verith man," Thomas told her. "I still haven't met him since he remained at the other hideout, waiting for... I'm sorry, I forget their names."

"Erin and Brighten," Riley finished. "Okay, let's go talk to the rest."

"Of course, my Savior." Thomas turned to open the door.

Riley smiled in resignation at his inability to remember her sole instruction. If she told him to go outside, take his pants off, and run around screaming like a lunatic he'd do it, no questions asked.

Not calling her a Savior? That was like pulling fucking teeth.

The two made their way downstairs. Riley found William sitting over a large plate of eggs and bacon. Eric was next to him, a much smaller plate in front of him.

Lucie was standing at the stove, still cooking. Her eyes were red, meaning she was doing something with magic. Riley didn't feel like asking what the hell was going on with that. She had enough to deal with.

"Glad you got up, lazy." William shoved a forkful of eggs into his mouth.

"Let's be honest, William. Your ass would still be asleep if there wasn't food out here. The only thing that moves you is food and...Well, Erin now." Riley grinned. She'd missed this banter.

William opened his mouth to talk, but it had too much food in it.

"All the better," Lucie said. "Just keep food in his mouth and he shuts up."

"Where's Kris? Where's Worth?" Riley asked as she looked around the kitchen.

"They're both still asleep. I think Worth is about as

hungover as he's ever been," Lucie answered, bringing over another plate of food. "Sit, girl. Eat."

Riley looked at the steaming eggs and bacon. "We need to discuss what to do first."

"You can eat and discuss. Just don't take as big of bites as the fat man over there."

"She ain't as smart as me." William took another bite. "She can't figure out how to talk and eat."

"Hush, chubby." Riley looked from William to Thomas. "Have you eaten?"

"I will eat after you."

"Oh, that's rich," William chuckled. "Riley eats first now. Look at you, big shot."

Riley shook her head and decided not to argue with Thomas. To do so would only make William talk more shit. She sat and started to eat. "What did the owner of the house say? Bruce?"

Thomas spoke. "As of now, he's okay with us staying."

"Have they started invading houses already?" Riley asked.

"Yeah," William grumbled. "They're not around here yet. They're working closer to the castle, but they've started."

Riley chewed, thinking. She knew what Rendal wanted: her. He knew she was here, but— "How can Rendal know I'm in the kingdom but not where I am?"

"Worth and I are to thank for that," Lucie answered. "He's been keeping up a shield for much of last night, and when he passed out, I took over."

"That explains your red eyes. You two are running shifts to make sure he can't find me?"

"That's right. It's not terribly hard, given the size of Sidnie and the fact that he probably isn't looking that often. We may actually be able to quit altogether, now that he's started this mess."

"Have we heard from Verith?" she asked.

"No. He left about an hour ago," Lucie told her. "We don't know how long it'll take. We didn't have any idea when to expect Erin and Brighten back."

Riley looked at Eric and William. Both were focusing on their food, clearly trying not to consider the worst scenario: that Erin wasn't coming back.

"Hey, chumps. That woman can beat both your asses, so quit looking so glum," Riley told them.

William raised his eyebrows, then looked at Eric. He grinned, realizing he needed to lift the kid's spirits. He slugged Eric in the shoulder. "Listen to the woman and cheer up. Also, that's the only time you'll ever hear me say listen to Riley. Usually it's a ridiculous thing to do."

Riley turned to Lucie. "What do you think I should do? If he's going to start hurting people—if he's *already* hurting people—I have to go to him, right?"

Lucie sighed. "You don't learn, do ya? You just keep doing what he wants. Worth told me he said you needed to stay with those underground people and you refused. That 'bout right?"

Riley just gave a slight nod.

"Well, my answer is simple, girl. No, you *don't* go to him. Let him do what he wants. You continue learning your craft. This Thomas over here, he's supposedly adept at magic. You got Worth and me and a huge damned house to practice in. If we want to, we can probably leave the kingdom and go out into the Badlands to practice."

Riley shook her head. "That's the exact same thing Worth said."

"Worth was right, girl," Lucie responded. "You're not ready for Rendal. Worth told me you've come a long way, but that just makes it more dangerous for you."

"How so?"

"You're more vulnerable now than you were before. You're more powerful, but you're more susceptible to listening to him," Lucie answered.

"No," Riley told her. "That's not true."

"You asked me for my opinion, and that's it. You need to train more so you're ready the next time you meet him." Lucie turned away from Riley, heading back to the stove.

Riley looked down at her plate. "People are going to die if I don't."

"People are going to die no matter what. Rendal's fuckin' insane." William pushed his empty plate away. "But I'm down for whatever. I owe him and his little sidekick a serious ass-kickin'."

Verith walked into the room just then, Erin and Brighten following.

"I think we need to talk," Verith said.

"Oh, really? Let me guess." Riley hadn't touched another bite. "More trouble?"

"That's right." Erin wore her usual smile, looking as if nothing in the world could bother her.

William was on his feet looking at Erin, making sure she had no wounds.

"I'm fine, dearest." Erin touched his shoulder as she

moved to her son and laid a light kiss on Eric's cheek. She pulled up a chair next to him. Lucie didn't pause, setting a plate down in front of her.

"We're doomed," Brighten said. He sat at the table too. "Where's Kris?"

"Still sleeping," Lucie answered, handing him a plate too.

He didn't so much as look at it. "They have weapons that shouldn't even be possible."

"You know who *doesn't* have a weapon?" Lucie asked. "That big oaf sittin' there. Lost his damned sword."

Riley shook her head, chuckling. "That's something we're going to have to remedy because you're not too good at hand-to-hand combat."

"Anytime you want to try me, skinny, you just let me know."

Riley looked at Brighten. "You don't know me, but my name is Riley. I briefly met your friend Kris a few hours ago. Your name is Brighten, right?"

Brighten nodded but didn't look up.

"I'm here to help. I'm going to fix this, I promise you that. That mage who's taking over your city? I've faced him more than once, and he hasn't been able to stop me yet."

Brighten looked over. "You faced him?"

Riley glanced at William. "You haven't been telling him about my triumphs, prick?"

He grinned. "I'm too busy with my own triumphs to worry about yours."

She turned back to Brighten. "Yeah, I've faced him, and I'll do it again, too. Gladly. We're going to stop what's happening here and we're going to kill him, okay? But I need you to tell me what kind of weapons he has."

"She can tell you." Brighten nodded to Erin.

Riley saw the problem. The kid was scared. *Really* scared, but she'd spoken with William and Lucie about him. He was good, and valuable to this mission. He was learning magic, and he knew the kingdom. He had senses that rivaled Riley's and William's.

She needed him to be part of this.

"I'd like to hear it from you," she told him.

"He's scared right now," Erin interjected, "but when we were at the castle, he was a fucking champion."

Brighten's eyes showed a little energy at her words.

"We escaped," Erin told him. "And we couldn't have done it without you. Scared or not, you know that."

He nodded, eyes down.

"So, Brighten," Riley continued. "Tell me about these weapons."

He nodded again, seeming to gain courage, and started speaking. "They're... I mean, everybody has heard stories about the weapons before the World's Worst Day Ever. The weapons from long ago. They resemble those."

"How so?" William asked, leaning forward.

"Well, to begin with, they're using mages to control them. The first thing we saw, these mages threw these orbs with their minds. The orbs flew across the room and released metal pellets. I think the word for them used to be 'bullets?' I'm not sure. But those pellets shot three people in cages and killed them all."

He looked up at Riley.

"The scary part isn't the pellets. It's that those mages

could throw those orbs from anywhere. They don't have to be next to you. They could sit in the castle and wield them, so we wouldn't really be killing the enemy. We'd only be killing the enemy's weapons."

"It'd be like we sent our swords out to fight for us," William mused. "The enemy might be able to destroy them, but we could just make more."

"Exactly," Brighten agreed. "And those were only the first weapons we saw. There's more stuff going on down there. A lot more."

"Let's hear it," Riley urged.

"They aren't all pellets. Some exploded. We saw them detonating things in certain parts of the tunnels. Those won't kill only a couple of people. They'll kill thousands."

"How were they detonating down there?" Riley asked.

"They were controlled detonations. Small things. Erin and I thought they were just getting the technology right, though. They could make the explosions *much* bigger," Brighten told her.

"So, he's creating an army that can be continually replaced?" Verith asked, speaking for the first time since entering.

Brighten nodded.

"They're all covered with the amphoralds, and that means they're all powered by human energy. The mages control them with their minds, but they get their energy from a magical human touching them," Erin said.

William stood up from the table. "If that comes to New Perth, we're in trouble. We still have magicals, even if most people think we don't."

"Gettin' scared now, chubby?" Riley jested.

"I'm just scared that *you're* gettin' scared, skinny. I'll take a million of those little orbs by myself." William winked and then started pacing. "But we do have to find a way to stop them from makin' more. That's as important as anything else we can do right now."

"It's not more important than stopping Rendal from pulling people out of their houses and executing them," Riley told him.

"You got the intelligence of a damned squirrel," William retorted.

"Can you even spell 'intelligence?'" Riley laughed.

He ignored her. "He can pull people out from their houses, torture them, and do anything else he wants. It's not good, I'll give you that—"

"It's evil," Riley corrected.

"Evil, fine. But he can't pull *everyone* out of their houses. If those damned orbs, the explodin' ones, get above New Perth, that's it. Kaput. Everything we love is fuckin' gone."

"He won't do that," Riley said. "He wants to *own* New Perth."

"He ain't gotta do it, Riley. He's only gotta *threaten* to do it. He only has to put 'em over the kingdom and the Prefect will give in. He can hold those things above New Perth forever, and then he owns New Perth forever." William shook his head while pacing. "No, we have to stop what he's doing down there. That's the most important thing."

Riley wanted to say something, but she couldn't think of an argument. He was right. Destroying those weapons was crucial.

William stopped and looked at her. "Cat got your

tongue, skinny? Or you just realizing I'm smarter than you?"

"We have to stop both," Riley told him. "The people from dying and those weapons from getting out. The question is how."

The room fell silent, everyone thinking through the issues.

Brighten finally spoke up. "We can destroy the weapons."

"How?" William asked.

Brighten shrugged. "Blow up the castle. You do that, all those tunnels and rooms are going down with it."

The room went silent again. They all stared at Brighten as if he had two heads.

Finally, it was Lucie who spoke. "Son, do you know what you're talkin' about doin'? I've never seen a building that size in my whole life, and you're talking about leveling it."

"You are asking how we can stop the weapons." Brighten looked around. "There are other ways, of course, but people are going to get hurt. *Us*, most likely. Because we'll have to go down there and start killin' folks. She and I made it out because there were only two of us. Everybody down there was runnin' around like their asses were on fire, and I used a little Psychic magic to help. You go down there lookin' to hurt folks, they're gonna hurt you back."

Riley saw it clearly. He wasn't wrong.

"And you're willing to bring down your kingdom's castle?" William asked.

Brighten shrugged again. "I'm willing to do what it takes to keep from letting those things out."

Riley looked at Verith. "Is it possible? Could we demolish something like that?"

Verith nodded. "Sure, it's possible. It'll be real tough, but you can blow up anything with the right materials. It's finding the materials and then getting them into the right spot that's the hard part."

"William," Riley started, "we're the highest ranking members of New Perth here besides Mason. If we bring the castle down, that *is* an act of war. We will basically be going to war with Sidnie."

William sighed. "I know."

"And there's Mason to consider," Riley continued. "I'm not doing anything to that castle if he's still in it, which from what it sounds like, he is."

"This is fuckin' ridiculous. Rendal's got our balls in a damn vice and there ain't no way to get 'em out." William huffed.

"As small as your balls are, you could put a little oil on 'em and slide 'em right out." Lucie chuckled.

"So now it's a twofold thing." Riley brought the conversation back on track. "We'd have to rescue Mason and *then* blow up the place."

"Do one right after the other," Verith interjected. "Set it up so that the explosives are in place, then right after the rescue, detonate."

"You make it sound pretty simple," Riley said.

"Well, it's a simple concept," Verith explained. "It's a much tougher implementation."

"We can't make this decision right now," Riley finally decided. "We need more time. There might be more options we're not seeing."

"There *isn't* much time," Brighten told her. "What we saw down there... They aren't in the beginning stages. They're moving along fast."

"Thomas!" It was Bruce's voice. The owner of the house. "Thomas, where the hell are you?"

Thomas was still in the kitchen, having kept his mouth shut the entire time, trusting Riley's decisions completely.

He opened the kitchen's door. "We're in here!"

The owner's feet could be heard pounding down the hallway. He opened the door without any ceremony. He was out of breath, his face flushed. "You need to see this. I think every single one of you needs to see this."

CHAPTER SEVEN

The crowd was thick, people standing shoulder to shoulder, and Riley knew that was exactly what the men with weapons had wanted.

The deeds were already done, the guards already left.

Despite what Bruce had said, Riley had decided that only a small group would go see what he was talking about: her and William, with Kris leading them.

Now the three of them stood on top of a building about a quarter mile away.

No way could William get down to the crowd of people.

They could see perfectly from that distance, although Riley half wished she couldn't.

"Do you see any more guards?" William asked.

Riley shook her head. "No, none. They're all gone."

"Good thing, too, because I wouldn't be able to stand here any longer if so. I'd have to go down and kill them."

A family lay dead on the street. Two children, two adults. They had been tossed from the top of the house, which was a tall one. These people weren't poor. They were wealthy.

"Rendal doesn't give one fuck," William said. "Not a single one."

Riley nodded. She didn't have any words.

Kris did, though. "That motherfucking piece-of-shit asshole. I'm no fan of rich kids or their asshole parents, but they didn't deserve this. I'm gonna take Rendal's nutsack, cut it open, and pour acid in it."

"The mouth on this one!" Riley cocked her head and looked at William.

"No manners, her, but she's right. Rendal deserves all of that and more."

Riley looked back at the massacre. "If they weren't scared before, they are now."

"But of who?" Kris asked. "First they tried to convince us there were spies, and now they're fucking killing their own citizens."

"Citizens who are hiding spies," Riley corrected. "Those people down there are scared of three separate things: first, the spies. Second, each other. They don't want to be ratted out, and they don't want to aid anyone 'helping' the spies. Third, they're scared of the guards, and in that order."

"They believe it? They believe those people had some-thing to do with fuckin' *spies*?" Kris asked.

"Those down there? Yeah, they do. Because they're staring at dead people. Other people might not yet, but they will as this continues. As it gets worse." Riley's mind was going back to what Rendal had told her.

He'd take everything.

Everything she loved. Everyone she cared for. He'd make everyone suffer until she came to his side.

And it was starting. She'd arrived, and he was making people suffer.

And those she loved? The scars forming on William's arms were proof that he was coming for them, too.

"We've got to do something, Riley," the big man whispered. "We've got to find a way to stop this. It's a damned massacre."

"We will." Riley nodded, her determination total. "We're gonna stop him, and he's going to wish he was never born before we're done."

"You ready?" Riley whispered.

"Born ready, little girl, but you already knew that," William answered.

The two stood outside one of the poorer houses in Sidnie. They couldn't stop everything that was happening, but after seeing the massacre earlier, they were going to send their own message back to Rendal.

We're here, and we're going to kick your ass.

The guards had gone into the house about five minutes ago. People were starting to gather on the streets, knowing what was happening inside. The family had been suspected of harboring spies.

They would give up the spies or die.

Riley and William knew the family had nothing to give up, so they would die.

Or they would have until the Right Hands decided to step in.

Both wore cloaks, Riley's sword hidden under hers.

"You going to be able to help much with that thing?" Riley grinned, not looking away from the house. She was talking about William's new weapon.

"How many guards went inside?" William asked.

"Twelve."

"I'll kill more with this mace than you will with that sword and your so-called 'new powers.'" The mace was hidden under his cloak, a massive thing with spikes on the ball at the end.

"I'll take that bet." Riley was glad to be with William again. She'd missed the back and forth. She'd missed *him*. "What's the wager?"

"Hmmm." William considered. "Bragging rights works for me."

"That's a deal," Riley responded.

A cry rang out from inside the house. The guards were done threatening now. It was time to get to the real reasons they'd come: murder and terror.

"Shall we?" William asked.

Riley shook her head. "One more minute. They're going to bring the family outside. These people need to see us beat their asses."

"Once in a rare while you say somethin' smart, skinny."

Another scream, then the first guard tossed a woman through the front door. She hit the pavement hard, scraping her arms and legs.

The husband was tossed out next, followed by a child no more than ten years old.

"Now?" William was clearly ready to get this show on the road.

"Wait," Riley commanded.

"Damn it, skinny." William knew she was right, though.

The guards flowed out from the house, forming a line in front of the gathering crowd.

"*These people are traitors to Sidnie!*" the head guard shouted. "They know where some New Perth spies are, and they're hiding them! We've given them a chance to talk, but they refuse!"

The woman shrieked, "It's not true! We don't know anything!"

The guard kicked her in the mouth.

"Okay, that'll do," Riley told William. "Let's finish these cretins."

"You're always tryin' to be proper." William removed his cloak. "Let's finish these fuckers."

Riley left her cloak on but removed her sword as William took his mace out.

"Hey!" he called. "I know where the spies are! Why don't ya come try to get it out of me?"

William's eyes lit red and fire erupted down his mace.

The guards looked stunned, not sure who was standing in front of them.

"Oh, shit," one of them finally whispered. "It's him. The spy."

William glanced at Riley. "My reputation precedes me. Don't seem like you got much of a reputation, skinny. Sucks to be you."

"We'll see who's got the reputation when this is done." Riley's mind snapped into place, the killer in her taking over. She saw all of the guards at once, down to tiny muscle movements.

Four on the left came forward.

Riley and William moved at the same time, each knowing exactly what the other would do.

Riley went toward the four, William to the others.

The guards spread out, trying to trap her in a circle. Riley let them.

She twirled her sword in front of her body, taking no defensive or offensive position, just waiting on them to squeeze the circle tighter.

"Is it her?" one of them asked as they approached.

"Got to be the bitch the mage is talkin' about," another answered.

"I'm that bitch," Riley assured them. "Come make yourselves famous."

She waited, the circle they'd formed getting tighter.

Now, she thought.

Her eyes lit and she put the point of her sword on the ground.

Riley leapt into the air as the first guard jabbed his weapon. She backflipped over the circle, landing on her feet. Her sword raced outward, her body controlling it with effortless precision.

She danced around the tight circle of men who had set themselves up perfectly to die. Her sword easily cut through the group, leaving them in a heap on the ground.

Riley turned to William.

He slammed one of the guard's heads with his mace, breaking the man's skull and setting his hair on fire at the same time.

"You're gonna lose the bet!" William shouted.

"To hell with that!" Riley rushed across the short distance separating the two of them.

William had dropped three already and the others were backing up, trying to figure out how to handle the giant who had fire blazing down his arm and weapon.

There were five left.

"Get outta here," William told her. "These are mine."

"We'll see."

William lunged.

Riley remained where she was, her eyes turning red. She touched her sword to the ground again. A trail of fire shot out, blitzing past William. It reached the first soldier and then split, rapidly forming a circle around the guards.

"Hey!" William shouted. "That's not fair!"

The fire finished creating its circle and rose high, engulfing the remaining men in mere seconds.

They screamed into the night air. The family that had been cast to the ground scrambled up, moving across the street to the rest of the crowd.

William turned to Riley. "That ain't fair. That wasn't part of the rules. You didn't win shit."

"Oh, the *rules*? I didn't see you post them anywhere, chubby," Riley replied with a grin.

She turned around, removing her cloak finally, and addressed the people staring at her and William.

"These men came here to hurt that family, saying they knew where I was. That family has never seen me before right now, and they know nothing of me. Those guards, who serve these rulers? They're evil, and they're doing this to scare you. I'm here to say you don't have to be scared.

JACE MITCHELL & MICHAEL ANDERLE

You don't have to worry about dying, because I'm going to kill that mage in his tower."

She stepped a bit closer to the crowd.

"My name is Riley Trident, and I'm a Right Hand of New Perth. We are not spies. We are here to liberate your city from the false ruler who has taken over. Spread *that* word, and do not fear these evil men. You should only fear that *you* might become evil, turning your neighbor in for something they did not do."

Riley looked at the hopeful faces, seeing the family that had nearly died huddled together. They were beyond grateful; no words were necessary to explain it.

"Tell that mage I'm coming for him and there's no place he can hide. There's nowhere he can run. He's already dead. He just doesn't know it yet."

"How many households?" Rendal asked.

"Ten, sir. That was during the daylight hours. We're going to hunt throughout the night, too," Harold answered.

"Has she stuck her head up yet?"

Harold swallowed. "Yes, sir. She killed the guards at one of the houses and saved the people."

Rendal gritted his teeth. "Were we not able to do *anything?*"

"No, sir." Harold shook his head.

Rendal tried to quiet his anger. This was what he had wanted: the killing of innocents to bring Riley into the open. They hadn't caught her *this* time, but it didn't mean they wouldn't the next.

He looked at Mason. The man was growing tired, his eyes slowly closing, although he'd jerk them open the moment he realized. Mason hated sleeping while Rendal was awake.

Rendal smiled, watching as Mason drifted into slumber. "Mason! How are ya, chap?"

The Assistant Prefect's eyes shot open, shock coming before the anger.

Rendal kept smiling. "I think you may see your precious Riley very soon."

Mason stared at him. "Only because she's a better person than you."

"Why would you say that, Mason? Have I not treated you relatively well? Sure, we've had some small problems, but what couple doesn't, you know?"

Mason closed his eyes again, although Rendal knew he was just ignoring him.

"It hurts," the mage continued, "that you think so poorly of me. These people dying—they serve a greater good." He looked at Harold. "Don't you think?"

"Yes, sir, that's true."

"See! Harold understands." Rendal was almost laughing now. The Assistant Prefect continued ignoring him. "These people who are dying, they're going to bring great peace to New Perth. Their deaths won't be in vain because they will bring Riley to me. And from there, both of us to New Perth."

"Yes, Rendal, you are a benevolent dictator. You bring peace and joy wherever you go." Mason didn't open his eyes as he spoke.

"There's the spirit." Rendal stood up and walked over to

the humidor. He hadn't paid it much attention until a day or so ago. Sidnie's Prefect kept it nicely stocked, however.

Or he had.

Now the Prefect just stood in the corner most of the day, sometimes drooling, sometimes not.

"Harold, would you like a cigar?" the mage asked.

"No, sir."

Rendal shrugged and picked a random one. He didn't have the first clue about them, but he should probably get used to trappings like this. After all, he was now royalty, and would be for the rest of his life.

He took the cigar back to his seat. He cut the end off, then used a match to light it. He was quiet as he puffed, enjoying the aroma as the smoke rose to the ceiling.

"Mason, we're going to be heading home soon. Are you looking forward to that?"

"You're going to be dead soon, Rendal. Are you looking forward to that?" The Assistant Prefect's face was calm.

"Beneath us right now are the weapons that are going to ensure New Perth can do nothing but surrender to me. I'm leaving nothing to chance. All my years in exile and all my years struggling are going to pay off very soon."

"Rendal, as much as I enjoy these chats, are they necessary?" Mason asked. "I'd much rather rest some since we're pals and all."

"Yes, unfortunately, they are necessary. I need to decide what to do with you. That's the one thing I'm confused about." Rendal took a drag from his cigar and blew the smoke out of his mouth, his eyes turning red as he did.

The smoke moved as the mage commanded, forming a replica of New Perth's castle.

The red in his eyes faded, and the smoke drifted into the air.

"You see, it's a conundrum. Riley is obsessed with you. She'd burn this whole kingdom to the ground to get you back, yet I *hate* you, Mason. I hate your insolence and your arrogance. I hate everything about you if I can be frank." Rendal spoke as if he were describing the taste of his cigar rather than deep-seated emotions.

"I assure you, the feeling is mutual," Mason responded.

"But the rub here is, killing you may not be possible, and I cannot *stand* that." Rendal shook his head. "So what do I do? Harold, do you have any ideas?"

His head guard stood at the room's door. "Sir, this is indeed a tough decision."

"You see, Mason, I wish I could just throw you right off the balcony out there. That would serve me perfectly well," Rendal waxed.

"Too bad you can't." Mason gave a small smirk.

"I know, I know." Rendal wasn't taking the bait, instead puffing at his cigar again.

And then it struck him—what he should do.

It came all at once, the idea hitting him like a bolt of lightning.

"Oh, that's wonderful," he whispered. "It's almost too perfect."

The room grew silent and Mason opened his eyes, staring at the mage.

Rendal slowly turned his head to the Assistant Prefect. "I've been dumb. Do you know that?"

"I've known it since the moment you decided you could take New Perth, Rendal," Mason answered.

"Oh, you and your insults. That's fine. I can't believe I didn't see this until now." Rendal looked at Harold. "I want you to drain him."

"Yes, sir," Harold answered.

"In public."

Mason slowly sat up.

"She's here, and I told her I would take everything from her," Rendal continued gleefully. "So let's start. If she wants to stay hidden and let people die, we'll go ahead and make her suffer too. Get Artino on it. Tell him to put Mason in a cage right outside the castle, and start draining him tomorrow morning."

"Fuck you, Rendal. It's not going to work." Mason didn't look as confident as he sounded, though.

"Oh, I think we both know it will. Look at how far she's come to get you back, my friend. I've been weak, and that's the truth. Not harming you? That was a mistake."

"Stand up," Harold told Mason.

The Assistant Prefect obeyed, getting to his feet.

"Let's go. Don't give me any problems and I won't have to hurt you, Mason."

The Assistant Prefect swallowed, his face going between fear and resolve.

Rendal smiled. "You see, dear sir, everything marches to my drum, and now you do too. Shout your insults from the cage. Maybe I'll hear them."

Mason's entire life had been about making him a leader; someone who would ensure the people of New Perth thrived and prospered. Yet, since Rendal took him, he'd been a slave, taken from leader to slave by this evil mage.

And now the slave was going to his death, or as close to it as he could get without actually dying.

Rendal had once before thrown Mason in with those he drained. They all looked moments away from turning into ghosts, as if all their energy had been sucked from their bodies.

Mason had been groomed to be a leader, not a slave, and as he was brought deep into the castle's bowels, he remembered that.

He wouldn't grovel to these people. He wouldn't beg. He wouldn't give any quarter.

Harold took him to the castle's first floor, then walked him through what felt like an unending tunnel.

Finally, he reached a massive room, one with more tunnels branching off it. People were *everywhere*, walking to and fro. All of them seemed to be intensely busy, none even looking at the new entrants.

"Follow me. Don't be dumb. If you try to run, you know I'm going to catch you, and you know I'm going to pummel you when I do."

"Did you willingly give your balls to Rendal?" Mason asked. "Or did he take them?"

Harold chuckled. "You New Perthians are fools. You see what the man is doing. Look right in front of you. All this work? It's producing weapons that you can't even imagine. He's going to rule this continent, and you idiots seem oblivious to that truth."

"No, we just have bigger balls than you," Mason told him. "My balls are so big it hurts to sit down sometimes, and that means Rendal can't take them. Even if I tried to give them away, he wouldn't be able to carry them. Yours, unfortunately, must have been much smaller. All the same, when Riley gets to you, she'll make sure they get stomped to nothing."

"Just shut up and follow me," Harold grumbled.

The two walked across the room, heading toward a short man wearing glasses.

"Artino—" Harold tried to say, but the short man was having nothing of it.

"Harold! Harold! We've had a security breach! I've been trying to tell you idiots that for the past six hours, but I can't pull myself away from my work. I've sent messages. Sent messengers. The guards were assaulted! Hurt badly, and that means someone came down here!"

Harold's eyes narrowed. Mason could tell that Harold finally realized that they'd passed no security guards on the way down here. "What do you mean, they were assaulted?"

"Are you listening to me, Harold? Someone attacked them! Broken bones! Someone got down here!" Artino was shrill, his face red and his glasses falling down his nose as he yelled.

"Who?"

"How am I to know, man? I'm not a guard. I'm a scientist, and my work is important! Rendal is running a shoddy operation up there! Someone got down here!"

Harold grew quiet for a second, and Mason could tell the man was holding in his anger. Harold did that a lot, rarely showing the rage that lived inside him.

Wait until William gets to you again, Mason thought. *You're going to want all of that rage—every last bit of it.*

"I'll figure it out," Harold finally said. "Is anything amiss?"

"How am I supposed to know, dolt? You see that I'm working. You see everything I'm dealing with! Look at all these people. I don't know half of them, but Rendal is always pushing, pushing, pushing, and now this operation is huge!"

Harold sighed, although Mason could see the rage beneath the surface. He didn't like being spoken to in such a manner by someone he considered beneath him.

"Calm down. I'll take care of it. But look, Rendal wants you to do something with him." Harold gestured toward Mason.

Artino's eyes finally moved to the man standing slightly behind Harold.

"Who is *this*?" Artino asked. "I don't have time for *more*."

"This is the Assistant Prefect of New Perth. He's *important*, Artino, both to Rendal and toward our goal."

Artino was too oblivious to anything outside of his own head to realize that Harold wanted to punch him right in the fucking face.

The scientist sighed. "What does Rendal want?"

"It shouldn't be complicated," Harold explained. "He wants you to drain him, but in public. Outside the castle."

"What do you know about what's complicated?" the scientist asked. "The most complicated thing you do is carry a sword and decide what part of someone's body to shove it into." He looked at Mason. "So *you're* the one Rendal wanted?"

It was the first time the scientist had appeared calm since they entered this room.

"Drain you, huh? This isn't about nanocytes, then. We're well-stocked, so Rendal told me to put our energies into these weapons." Artino nodded and looked at Harold. "This is about *her*, isn't it? Draining him in public is about getting the Right Hand? Rendal tells me nothing, just pushes and pushes but pulls me away from my work almost constantly. But this! He's hoping to get *her*, isn't he?"

"That's not your concern," Harold responded. "You follow orders just like the rest of us. You get him in a cage and drain him. That's all you need to know."

Artino waved his hand as if dismissing Harold. "He's pulling me away from my work with this, but it might be worth it. If we get her, I might be able to actually focus without all his interruptions."

He took another step closer to Mason.

"Well, Assistant Prefect, I doubt you thought this would be your destiny, but it's not so bad. You will be contributing to a much larger goal, one that's going to change the world." The scientist smiled, and Mason realized he was just as crazy as everyone else in this organization.

He might not be as violent, but the man was nuts.

"Harold," Mason said, "I didn't think it was possible, but I've found someone more pathetic than you. This asshat sits down here creating weapons to kill people while sacrificing nothing."

Harold chuckled but said nothing.

Artino looked at Mason narrowly. "It didn't *have* to hurt, Assistant Prefect, but now it will."

"And, *Artino*," Mason responded, "it's going to hurt when Riley gets hold of you. Whatever you're about to do to me, it'll be mere drops in the bucket that Riley's got in store for you."

"Come on," Kris told Brighten. "I can't stand bein' inside this place anymore. We gotta get out."

Brighten raised an eyebrow and looked at his friend. "You really do have a death wish. I don't, however. I ain't goin' nowhere until that stupid school tonight."

Kris didn't care what he said; she rarely did. She'd hardly been able to leave the hideout for days and days, all because that damn mage had caught her.

She couldn't take it anymore, though. 'I'm losin' my mind in here. Let's go to the town square and see if we can steal anything."

Brighten shook his head. "Nope. Not doin' it. I've had just about enough danger for now, and I *know* Riley and them are gonna ask me to do somethin' soon. Somethin' I don't wanna do."

"Look." Kris walked over to his chair. "I'm goin', and if you let me go by myself, you're a shit friend.'

She grinned, knowing what she was doing.

Brighten rolled his eyes. "Not gonna work."

"If someone sees me or catches me and I get picked up, I'll need you there to make sure that everyone here knows I've been captured."

"Or you could not be a moron and not leave the house," Brighten responded. "Plus, we've been waiting on digs like this. This is a *rich* person's house, and we can do whatever we want here. You're living in the lap of luxury. You should enjoy it."

Kris shook her head, still smiling. "Nope. We're goin' to steal some stuff. Now let's go."

She turned and started walking toward the house's front door, not looking to see if Brighten was following.

Finally, she heard his chair moving back. "This is *dumb*, Kris."

She smiled. "Maybe, but I'm goin' stir-crazy. Come on, we don't have to pickpocket anybody, but let's just get some fresh air."

He caught up with her. "It's not right, you using our friendship against me."

"Since when did I base my life off doin' things that are right, numbnuts?" Kris asked. "Plus, all the new magic you got now, you should be able to get us out of any scrapes we find ourselves in."

"And if Riley or William finds out we left? They're goin' to raise hell," Brighten protested.

"They ain't gonna find out. No one's gonna find out. Erin's been runnin' around tellin' everyone how brave you are, but you sound like the same scaredy-cat as always to me."

Brighten sighed. "Fuck it. Let's go. Maybe you will get caught by a guard and I won't have to put up with you anymore. That's about as good as anyone can hope for at this point."

"You'd miss me," Kris responded, then opened the door.

They snuck out quietly, the house too big for anyone to notice if they weren't specifically looking for the two.

They didn't say much as they walked toward kingdom's

square. While they hadn't hung out much in this part of the city—the wealthy part—they both knew how to get to the square with their eyes closed.

It was where all the marks were every single day, and although a lot had changed in Sidnie, *that* hadn't.

"Something's going on," Brighten observed as they got closer.

Kris thought he was right. They weren't even at the square yet, but a lot of people were walking toward it. It was still somewhat early in the morning, and that made the number of people that much more unusual.

"It can't be good," Brighten commented. "Nothing good happens in the square anymore." He looked at Kris. "Let's go back."

"No way, numbnuts. We're already here. No sense in turning around." She didn't look at him, knowing even that would give him a chance to slow down.

About five minutes later, they got to the square.

Both stopped and stared.

The place was *packed*. Hundreds of people were here, and none of them were shopping. The merchants had ceased trying to sell their goods and were standing with the rest of the crowd.

At the center of the square, guards stood in a box formation, shoulder to shoulder looking out.

A pole had been erected in the middle of their box, jutting up twenty feet into the air. A *cage* had been installed around the top of it, with the pole going through the middle and connecting with the top.

A man sat in the corner of that cage.

Wires or tubes were hooked to the man; Kris couldn't

be sure which. Each tube was inserted into his skin; the tubes were black, so Kris couldn't see whether blood was being drained or some substance was flowing into the man.

A small box sat in the cage, and all the tubes connected to it. The box had a green amphorald on top, which was shining brightly. That box was doing *something*, although Kris didn't have the first clue as to what.

"I told you," Brighten whispered. "I told you we had no business leavin' the house."

"Hush. Let's get closer." Kris didn't wait for him to respond but started working her way through the crowd of people. Brighten followed quickly, their old habits taking over. No one noticed the two kids moving among them, and no one looked down. They almost didn't exist—and six weeks ago, if a crowd like this had gathered, Kris and Brighten would have made off with *a lot* of money.

Kris wasn't concerned with wealth right now, though.

The man in the cage. He held her attention.

"You think it's him?" she asked Brighten as they passed a huge blacksmith.

"I don't know. I hope not, for everyone's sake. Riley will unleash holy hell on these people," Brighten answered.

The "him" Kris was referring to was New Perth's Assistant Prefect. Kris and Brighten had both been briefed on him since he was the main reason these New Perthians had come here: to retrieve him.

"No farther," Brighten cautioned, grabbing Kris's arm.

She listened to him and stopped. They could see everything they needed from here.

The man was sweating, and he looked to be in a lot of

pain. Whatever was happening with those wires wasn't a good time, Kris felt sure of that.

"Who is that?" Kris asked a woman to her left. She put on her "kid" voice, one that adults took to mean she was lost and needed guidance. It usually worked well with marks when she needed to direct their attention elsewhere.

"One of the spies," the woman spoke gruffly. She was clearly angry; she didn't look away from the cage. "They threw him up there this morning. Supposedly he's some royalty from New Perth. They found him in one of the raids they been doin' on the houses."

"What are all those tubes on him?" Kris asked.

The woman shook her head. "I ain't sure. Rumor says it's truth serum; something to make him tell where the rest of his kind are. I'm ready to get this war goin'. Show these New Perth assholes they can't do whatever they want."

Someone chucked what looked to be a rotten head of lettuce at the cage. It hit one of the bars and broke apart, and some of the leaves flew through and hit the man.

Another person slung an apple, and this one shot through the bars, hitting the Assistant Prefect squarely in the chest. He grimaced but made no noise.

Kris looked at Brighten. His face was nearly white as he stared up at the caged man.

"We need to go back," she told him. "We have to tell Riley."

"*Now* you want to go back? I didn't want to come here in the first place."

"Yeah, well, we're lucky I'm brave instead of a scared-ass like you or no one would know," Kris shot back. "Come on, let's get the hell out of here."

The two wound their way out of the crowd, heading back the way they'd come.

Kris couldn't help herself as she left. Or rather, her hands couldn't. They dipped into a few pockets, pulling out wallets and coins.

It was okay; no one noticed. Plus, all those jackasses were believing the bullshit in front of them: that the man up there was a spy instead of a victim. Nah, Kris was glad she'd made herself richer off those morons.

Truth be told, a few missing coins shouldn't worry them. If that man up there was indeed the Assistant Prefect, they should be concerned about Riley's wrath.

CHAPTER EIGHT

R iley listened to the kids talking, anger growing inside her like some savage animal.

Their words were mere background noise now.

The important things had already been said.

Mason was in a cage, captive in the kingdom square, with people watching him like some common criminal. Being laughed at, jeered at.

"What were those tubes?" Erin asked.

"Rendal is draining him," Lucie answered. Her voice was grave.

Riley stopped pacing. "Draining him?"

Lucie nodded. "Yes. It's why Rendal is so powerful. It's what Pat originally told us about. He's draining the parts of Mason that allow you and me to practice magic. Mason can't practice it, but he still has the underlying ability. Rendal is taking it from him."

"What happens if he finishes? If he takes all of it out of Mason?"

Lucie shrugged. "I'm not sure. Pat lived, and he'd been

in Rendal's clutches a long time, but when Rendal had me, I saw people die from it. I think it depends on how much is taken. Perhaps the body depends on it now, or maybe they just drain too much blood. I can't say for certain."

Riley closed her eyes and gripped her sword's handle.

"I'm going to the square right now and freeing him."

"No you're not, skinny," William finally spoke up. He'd listened to the entire conversation, keeping quiet as everyone else talked. "Why do you think he's got Mason up there, Riley? He could have drained him in private. You're supposed to be smart, but you don't sound like it now."

"I don't care *why* he has him up there. He's got him in a cage, and people are pelting him with fucking *fruit!*"

William nodded. "I know. I heard the same things as you. Nothing else Rendal tried is working, so this is his last attempt. He's desperate; that's why he's using Mason. He wants you badly now, probably because you're using magic. Going to him is stupid."

Lucie raised her eyebrows. "Did someone kidnap William and put a person with a lick of intelligence in his place?"

"Ask Riley there what I can do with this mace," William responded. "Keep yappin', and I'll show you myself."

"Yeah, yeah," Lucie said. "But he's right, Riley. You go out there to get Mason and you're gone, simple as that. He might not let you back out this time. He hasn't thrown one of those necklaces on you, but if he does, you won't be usin' none of your magic against him. I promise you that."

"Then what the fuck *do* we do?" Riley asked. She was beyond frustrated.

"We stay the course." Verith stepped forward. "This

doesn't change anything besides our timeline. If he's being drained in public, we need to get things moving faster. We've got to lay the groundwork for bringing the castle down. This may actually make things easier."

"How's that?" William asked.

"Mason isn't in the castle, so we don't have to worry about getting him *out*. Rendal did that for us."

"How close are we to having the castle laced with explosives?" Riley still gripped her sword, her anger not dissipating.

"I have the explosives." Erin grinned.

William turned to her. "How did you get them?"

"Oh, I've got my ways." Erin winked. "Not everyone in the army buys the shit Rendal is selling. I've met some people who are on our side, even if they don't know exactly who we are."

"So what's next?" Riley asked.

Verith looked at Lucie. "How long does it take to drain someone?"

"I can't say for certain," Lucie pondered. "I'd imagine it depends on a lot of factors: the individual's strength, and how fast they're draining him. I mean, I can't even guess."

Riley was done with the conversation. It was time to take control. Time to get Mason back.

"Then we'll go off the assumption that he has a few days at most before we'll be looking at a skeleton in that damned cage." She turned to Verith. "Can you do it? Can you bring the castle down?"

He nodded. "It won't be easy, and I'll need everyone's help, but it should be possible."

Brighten swallowed. Riley could tell he wanted to offer some kind of protest, but he managed to keep it inside.

"All right, then," Riley told the group. "Our Assistant Prefect is in danger, and we've got fucking work to do. Verith, you're in charge. And everyone in here, you're going to listen to him. He tells you to jump, you ask 'how high?'"

Everyone nodded in agreement.

"Excuse me," Riley whispered and left the room.

She wanted to be alone, even though she knew she would be needed shortly. She had to get herself under control. She'd kept her rage from overflowing in front of them, but that didn't mean she could keep it at bay forever.

Riley headed downstairs, going to the basement where she and Eric practiced their sword work.

She reached the bottom of the stairs and felt her hands shaking.

A few moments later, William's loud footfalls filled the basement.

Riley turned around and saw him coming down the stairs.

"What?" she asked angrily.

William smiled but didn't stop. "Always so mean to me, and I'm nothin' but sweet to you all the time."

Riley turned back around, anger filling her eyes with tears.

"What's botherin' ya, skinny?" William asked as he reached the basement.

"Are you fucking *kidding* me right now?" Riley couldn't believe the question. "Mason is being *drained* in *public*. What do you *think* is wrong with me?"

"You're forgettin' who ya are, Riley. You're letting Rendal control your emotions, and that's exactly what he wants."

"Well, then he's getting it, because all I want to do is bring that damned castle down by myself." Riley's hands were balled into fists.

"I ain't been right this whole time." William remained near the bottom step, not getting closer to Riley. "I probably wasn't right about goin' to the ship back on that island. I've probably been too aggressive about a lot of this, but I can afford to be. Rendal just wants to kill me. He wants to *use* you, so you've gotta be smarter than that."

She whipped around. "You don't think I've been smart?"

He shrugged, grinning. "You brought your violence with you, that's for sure, but you might have left some of your brains back in New Perth. I mean, for goodness's sake, Riley! You left the damn kingdom thinking that would keep Rendal from attacking. Does that appear smart, looking back now?"

Riley let her hands relax. It seemed ridiculous that she'd done that, and if she were honest, *that* was what had caused Mason's kidnapping.

"And Worth told you to stay out in the desert, but here you are," William continued. "I'm not going to judge that too harshly one way or the other, but it seems like maybe he was right. Because now you're here, and Rendal knows it. What did he do? He threw Mason in a cage and started *draining* him, whatever the fuck that means."

"So what are you saying?" Riley asked. "That I should just not go after this damned mage who is bent on killing everyone?"

William chuckled. "I really do fear for him when you finally have the power to kill him. That sonofabitch is in for a terror he isn't expecting." He shook his head. "No, I'm not saying you should let him kill everyone and not try to stop him. That's not what we do as Right Hands. What I'm saying is that you and I have been wrong about much of this; that going in headfirst isn't *working*."

Riley just looked at William, unsure what to say.

"Mason isn't weak. We both know that. He's endured Rendal for weeks, so he's not going to keel over and die because they're draining blood from him or whatever the hell they're doing. He can last a couple of days, I'm sure of that. Let Verith do his thing. Let him bring down the castle."

William stopped talking for a second and smiled widely.

"Plus, I think there's some stuff we can do in the meantime that might make you a bit happier."

Riley's eyes narrowed. "Like what?"

"Just trust me." With that, William winked and started back up the stairs.

They waited until nightfall, and they brought Thomas with them.

"I'd rather bring Worth," William said.

"Hey, this is your idea," Riley told him. "Between the two of them, Thomas has a better mastery of Psychic magic. If we want this to work, we need him."

"See?" William grumbled. "You should have stayed out

in the desert. Then you could have learned what ya needed to and not have saddled me with this asshat."

"My Savior, is it necessary that he continue existing?" Thomas asked. "I could kill him easily if you're okay with it."

Riley laughed. "Yes, his existence is necessary."

"I wish he would try to kill me," William retorted. "It'd be the last thing he ever tried, I guarantee that."

"Okay, you two hush it," Riley commanded. "All this nonsense is going to get us caught."

The streets were mostly empty as the three moved through them. It was a risk for William to be out here, but he had decided to take it.

The streets were empty because no one wanted to be seen by a guard. The citizenry was terrified of anyone even possibly thinking they might have something to do with the New Perthian spies.

Hiding inside, especially at night, helped ensure their safety.

Brighten and Kris had explained to Riley where to go. They knew the kingdom square like the back of their hands, so it was easy for them to draw out a relatively detailed map.

Riley knew that Verith needed them for other things tonight, so bringing them on this mission hadn't been feasible.

They found the building easily, the kids' directions flawless.

"You first," William said.

They were at the back of the building and a ladder was

attached to the wall, allowing the proprietor to get to the roof whenever he wanted.

"Thomas the Asshat is going last," William continued. "If I fall, I want to land on him."

"If you fall," Thomas said, "we won't have to worry about blowing up the castle. You'll bring the whole city down with your fat ass."

Riley chuckled.

"That's funny, huh?" William asked.

"Yeah, he wins that round." She started up the ladder before William could say anything else.

The three of them climbed to the roof.

Riley could see Mason with no trouble. Four large fires burned around the cage and those standing guard. They lit everything up perfectly so that the entire city could see.

Just like Rendal wanted.

"He doesn't look good," Riley whispered.

"Hell, we probably don't look good either," William responded. "Or *you* don't look good. I do, of course. But my point is, it's been a trying time for everybody. It might not have anything to do with that cage and the draining."

Riley knew William was trying to make her feel better. Mason was clearly feeling the draining. His skin was pale, and sweat slicked his face.

There looked to be a jug of water in the cage's corner, so at least they were giving him liquids.

"All right, magic man. Prove your worth, or I'm going to toss you off the building." William winked at Riley, although Thomas couldn't see it.

"*Try* to throw me off the building. My Savior, are you ready?"

Riley shook her head at the title. "Yeah, go ahead, Thomas. And just call me Riley."

Thomas's eyes lit red as he reached out to Mason.

Riley *really* needed to learn Psychic Magic. She thought that in some ways, it was the most powerful of all the forms.

"What are you saying?" she asked.

But she hadn't needed to.

Mason's eyes focused on their building almost immediately. He started to stand, but quickly froze, then sat back down. His eyes never left them, though.

"He sees us," she whispered.

"Yes. I told him we're here."

"You can read his mind?" Riley asked Thomas.

"Yes. We can converse."

"What's he saying?" She could barely contain her excitement.

Thomas gave a slight smirk. "He said William looks like he's put on fifty pounds since the last time he saw the Right Hand."

William's head snapped to Thomas. "No, he didn't!"

Thomas nodded. "Sure did."

"Tell him we're going to save him," Riley instructed. "Tell him he just has to hold on for a few more days."

Thomas was quiet for a second as he passed on the information, then he said, "The Assistant Prefect told you to take your time. He's enjoying the view as well while having his blood drained."

Now Riley turned to Thomas. "Tell him to quit being a smartass."

Thomas nodded. "Mason says if that's the case, you two

need to get off your asses and come save him, because if you hadn't noticed, he's dying."

William chuckled and shook his head. "At least his spirits are up."

"Tell him we're working on it," Riley commanded. "Tell him if he doesn't quit being a jackass, we may just leave him in there and save the rest of the kingdom."

"Yes, my Savior."

A few more seconds passed, and then Thomas looked at Riley, his eyes still red. "He says you have to be careful. Both of you, although *I* would be okay if William wasn't so careful. He says Rendal's power is growing, and not just his magic. He's controlling everyone and everything. He has everything planned out."

Riley nodded. "Let him know that we have some plans Rendal isn't ready for, and that we're coming to get him."

Thomas nodded again, turning once more to the cage.

"Mason says to be careful, my Savior. He says to remember that his life is not as important as New Perth and that if he has to die here, so be it. It's your job to get back to New Perth and prepare the kingdom for the coming of this madman."

"We will do both," Riley responded.

Thomas continued, "He says that you can't simply come and get him right now. He thinks the cage is rigged, and if you try to get him out? He doesn't know exactly what will happen, but Rendal will somehow be alerted. He'll know."

Riley sighed. "Okay. Tell him we're going to wait, although it's not what I *want* to do."

William grinned. "Also tell him I've got a good decoy

for when we save him. We'll throw you in that cage instead, and no one will even know."

Thomas only looked at the Right Hand, his face not showing a hint of amusement. "I'd put you in it, but I'm certain the metal would break and you'd be sprawled in the street like a drunk."

Riley laughed, looking back toward the cage. She focused on the sentries beneath. "I sort of want to fuck with them."

"Probably not wise," William responded, "but when has that stopped you before?"

"Hmmm…" Riley didn't want to kill them, at least not right now. That would be too great a risk. "Come on," she said.

She darted to the ladder and started down. The men looked at each other for a second, united in their confusion, and followed her down.

Riley hit the ground and whisked around to the other side of the building.

She heard William and Thomas approach but put her index finger to her lips before they could say anything. They had to be absolutely silent here, or they would end up having to kill the sentries.

Riley's eyes turned red, and she knelt. This wasn't something the queen had taught her, or Worth, or anyone else. She was trying something completely new here, and she didn't know if it would work.

Riley put her palm on a cobblestone and concentrated.

Moments passed with nothing happening, but that only made Riley concentrate harder. She could do this. She had it in her; she knew it.

A light drizzle began to fall.

"Is that—"

Riley lifted a single finger at William's question, telling him to be quiet.

The drizzle grew stronger, rain falling in earnest.

Riley stared at the ground, focusing on what she wanted.

Freeze, she commanded.

Riley watched as the water around her hand turned to ice and then *spread.* The ice trailed toward the square, the falling rain freezing nearly as soon as it touched the ground.

"What the..." one of the sentries shouted, seeing the frozen water coming for them.

Riley didn't stop, not until she knew for certain the ice had reached them.

"*FUCK!*" one of them shouted, then Riley heard the thud of him landing on the ground. "my arm!"

"HA!" Another laughed, but that quickly turned into a scream when he fell to the cobblestones as well.

Riley didn't need to look at them to know they were all slipping and sliding. Perhaps one of them would break a fucking bone. That'd be nice.

She turned to the men with her, grinning wildly. "Okay, let's go see what's happening at the house."

"The castle is a hexagon," Verith told the group around him.

"You know what that is, Kris?" Brighten grinned. "It's a

bit tougher than reaching into someone's pocket and stealing, so I'm not sure you understand."

"I understand I'll kick you in the balls until your face turns blue if you don't shut your mouth," Kris responded.

Brighten kept grinning, but he didn't say another word. No one was quite sure Kris wouldn't do it.

Worth and Erin stood at the table with Verith and the kids. They were all looking down at a map of the castle that Brighten and Kris had drawn.

"Six sides," Verith kept going as if they'd said nothing. "Six corners. The explosives need to be on those six corners." He quickly dotted the map with his fingers. "These spots."

He looked at the four of them. "You four are going to pair up. Worth with Kris, Erin with Brighten. You'll each put explosives at two corners. I'll handle the other two."

"Well, that seems simple enough." Erin smiled, radiating her usual positivity.

"Yeah, super simple," Brighten grumbled. "Just march in with a bunch of explosives in our hands and drop them at the castle. No one should notice."

"All them brains and not a lick of imagination," Kris told him. She looked at Verith. "We can do it. We just need an excuse for why we're in there carrying bags."

"Well, Brighten and Erin don't need excuses, which is one of the reasons I'm putting them together. You and Worth...you're going to need *something*. I just don't know what," Verith answered.

"Worth know."

All eyes went to the man who'd been largely missing in

action for the past few days. Brighten and Kris hardly knew him.

"Well, don't hold out on us. What are we going to do?"

Worth smiled. "Same thing mage did. We lie."

"It's that simple, huh?" Brighten asked.

"Yeah." Kris shook her head. "Maybe someone should give him some more booze and let him go back to sleep. Let the adults finish talking."

Worth looked at Kris. "She Worth partner, aye?"

"Aye," Verith agreed. He trusted the tent man and wasn't going to discount anything he said.

"Good." Worth nodded. "She help with lies."

"What the hell is he talking about?" Kris asked Verith.

"When we start?" Worth asked, ignoring Kris's question.

"Tonight," Verith answered. "Erin and Brighten are dropping theirs off before they hit their jobs. I'm going to drop mine off tomorrow night. You two are supposed to go tonight as well, but I suppose that depends on your plan, Worth."

"We go tomorrow morning. Leave girl with Worth. Plan work fine."

Verith studied the bald man for a moment, as did everyone else around the table.

"Well," Erin finally said, "you going to tell us any more about it?"

Worth shook his head. "No. Leave girl. We be okay. You take care your piece. By end of day tomorrow, our explosives in place."

"I don't like the sound of this one bit," Kris commented. "This drunk is gonna end up getting me killed."

"Worth," Verith said. "She'll be *recognized*. The guards know her. Rendal knows her. It might be best that you leave her here and go alone."

Worth shook his head. "No. Trust Worth. She be fine. Need her to make it work."

Verith shrugged. "All right, kid. You're in Worth's care now. Best of luck."

Kris looked at Brighten, who was grinning. "What's so funny?"

"Nothing." His grin grew wider.

"Don't worry, numbnuts, I'm not scared. Whatever this drunk throws at me, I can handle."

Worth slapped her on the back *hard*, and she jumped forward.

"*That good spirit!*" Worth shouted. "No fear. We be fine!"

Brighten was still grinning, and Kris suddenly felt a cold brick in her stomach.

The drunk might just be crazy.

"Gooooood luck!" Brighten sang.

CHAPTER NINE

B righten and Erin decided to split up since both going to each point of the castle would take longer. Even if they would be combining forces, neither of them wanted to be around any longer than they had to.

For all intents and purposes, both were done with the school and military training after tonight.

For all intents and purposes, the school and military training would be over in a day or two anyway. Neither would exist anymore.

"Which corner do you want?" Erin had asked him.

Brighten had looked at the map. He knew which corner was closest for both of them, and everyone expected him to choose that one because he was scared. Because he didn't have the heart everyone else in this endeavor did.

Yet, he was one of only two who had gone into the bowels of the castle and come out alive.

Everyone thought he was scared because he was always talking about being scared.

He didn't have to be now.

He had pointed to the corner farthest away. "That one."

Erin peered at him with her eyebrows slightly raised. "You sure?"

Brighten nodded. "Positive."

Now, sitting in class and waiting for the damned thing to be over, he didn't *feel* positive. He knew how far away it was.

"What's wrong with you?" Lionel asked. Lionel was the boy Brighten had met on day one in this damned school, and he still knew Brighten as Jenkins.

All the same, Brighten liked Lionel. He was a good kid, good with magic, and didn't fully trust Rendal even though he was willingly learning everything the man taught.

"Just not feeling well," Brighten answered. That wasn't a lie. Brighten felt like he might puke right here in his chair. The night's session was ending, and Rendal was recapping what they'd learned.

"You don't look it, man," Lionel told him. "You look like you might fall over if you try to stand up. What's in the bag? You've never brought one before."

Brighten had been dreading that question since he walked into the building.

"I'm heading over to a friend's when I get done here, so it's just clothes and stuff." A ludicrous statement for anyone who knew Brighten, but it seemed to work.

Lionel only nodded. "I'm ready to go home. My parents are *pissed* that he's holding class this late every night, but... Well, nobody's going to say shit about it, ya know?"

Brighten nodded. He was ready to be out of here too, but then again, he didn't want to leave. He wished he could find some way to simply disappear so fast that a vacuum formed where he should have been sitting.

Alas, class ended.

"Until tomorrow, chap," Lionel said, the same send-off he offered every night.

"Unless Rendal the Great decides to send us to war," Brighten added sarcastically.

Brighten left the class. He saw that Erin's training was ending as well, people flowing out of the grounds. He caught sight of her easily enough but made no motion to go to her. This was on him.

I'm an idiot, he thought. *I should have taken the closer one.*

Too late for that, though.

Brighten slunk away from the crowd, his bag on his back. It'd be different if these *were* clothes, or books, or anything else. Instead, he had explosives in it, explosives he didn't understand at-fucking-all, and he had to sneak around the castle again despite the raised awareness, unload the explosives in a way that wouldn't be discovered, *hide* them, and get out without being noticed.

No problem, he thought sarcastically. *Just a walk in the park.*

Enough thinking, he chastised himself.

He got moving. The grounds were dark, and he *was* getting better at Psychic Magic. He let his mind flow in front of him, searching for possible sentries. He immediately saw twenty of them.

More than normal.

Fuck, he complained inside his head.

The entire kingdom was growing more alert, but right now he couldn't do shit about it.

He moved along the walkways, his mind always out in front of him. When guards came his way, he ducked into the darkness, shrouding himself with shadows and his mind the best he could.

Long minutes passed as he slowly made his way around the castle. He wondered if Erin was doing the same or if she was already finished.

Finally, he was within sight of the corner he needed.

And damn it if there wasn't a group of sentries standing there.

"What the hell?" he whispered to himself from his place of concealment.

There was no reason for them to be standing there. He'd felt them earlier but had hoped they would dispatch.

Of course, they hadn't. That was Brighten's luck. If Kris had been here, those guards would have left long ago, but not before rolling out a red carpet for her to walk across and kindly leaving a little picnic for her to eat after she was finished depositing her explosives.

Not Brighten, though.

No, everything had to be fucking tough.

You're tougher.

It was Erin's voice. Not her *actual* voice, but his memory of it.

You're tougher than those dumbass guards. Don't forget it. We need you. Now be tough and do your job.

Brighten nodded to himself.

He couldn't very well walk up there and ask them to kindly depart; he doubted that would go very well.

He sat, placing his bag in between his legs, and waited.

Minutes stretched into an hour.

The sonsofbitches didn't move. From what Brighten could tell, these were the laziest bastards in the whole kingdom, just sitting around shooting the shit the entire night.

Brighten kept waiting.

Another hour at least.

If this kept on this way, the sun would be up before too long.

"I've gotta do somethin'," he said aloud.

But what?

He only had one choice. Use magic.

Brighten stood, his hands shaking, but he focused.

You're tougher than these asshats, he heard Erin telling him again. *Always remember, you're the toughest prick in this whole castle.*

Brighten stepped out of the darkness. The guards still didn't see him, but they would soon enough.

He went forward, the bag on his back.

"What the hell ya doin', kid?" the tallest sentry asked as Brighten walked up to them.

There were four.

"I'm wonderin' the same thing about you all. Rendal sent me down here to check and see who was doin' what, and I've been watching you for hours. You ain't doin' shit but standing here holdin' each other's dicks." Brighten's eyes turned red as he spoke.

He ventured into their minds, trying to reinforce his words with an authority he didn't feel.

"Rendal?" one of the guards asked, sounding unsure.

"Yeah, *Rendal*," Brighten responded, his words filling the air and their heads. "And now I gotta go back and tell him you morons been hiding here doin' nothin' all night."

"What's that bag?" a guard asked. Brighten's magic clearly wasn't working as well on him.

"That bag's none of your damn concern," Brighten shot back. "Your only concern is how much trouble I'm about to get you in. You all need to get back to your posts right *now.*"

He saw doubt in all their eyes. He was clouding their vision of his eyes so that they couldn't see the redness in them. They didn't *want* to believe this pre-teen kid, but he seemed so *convincing.*

"Go on, now. Get!" he shouted at them.

They all looked at the ground, ashamed and embarrassed.

"Don't... We was just taking a break, is all. Don't get us in trouble, please," one of the men pleaded.

"I'll think about it," Brighten answered.

He watched as they started walking away, heading down the cobblestone pathway.

That was easy as hell, he thought.

His eyes were still red; he wasn't about to let the magic stop working.

One of the men stopped, and Brighten's stomach rose all the way to his throat. He couldn't say a damn word.

The man turned around, the one who had questioned the bag moments before.

He didn't look up as he spoke, as if he wanted to avoid Brighten's own eyes. "What's in that bag, kid?"

His voice was arctic ice.

"I-I-I just told you all to get!" Brighten tried to shout, but his voice cracked on the last word.

The spell was breaking, his hold over their minds slipping, and he felt it.

The rest turned around too.

"That damn mage ain't send you nowhere, did he?" the tall one asked. "Who the hell are you, and what's in that damned bag?"

"Oh, fuck," Brighten whispered. The red in his eyes faded.

He only had one option: *run!*

Yet his feet didn't move.

You're tougher than them. It was Erin's voice again, bright in his mind.

The four started walking toward him, one pulling out a black club.

"I don't know what the hell you think you're doin' down here, but I know for a fact it ain't no good. We'll find out what's what, though, real fast-like." The tall guard took the lead.

Brighten didn't move. "Go ahead and a lay a fu-fucking hand on me. Rendal will have all your asses in that cage next to the spy!"

He knew he sounded like a child, but he didn't move.

Even when the four reached him, their clubs out and ready to break his bones, Brighten stood firm. "I'm telling you ruh-right now to get the hell outta here!"

One of the guards laughed. "If I knew I got to beat up snot-nosed brats by hiding out, I'd do it every damned night."

He raised his club.

The shadow moved then. Brighten hadn't seen it before despite his well-above-average senses.

It moved with a speed he had not thought possible. Not even Erin in the tunnel compared to this.

The man raising his club was suddenly knocked off his feet, his mouth open to scream but no words escaping.

The other three turned away from Brighten, focusing on the shadow they could hardly see. It moved almost *through* them as if it had no form—no substance.

One.

Two.

Three.

They all dropped to the ground, either dead or unconscious.

The shadow turned toward Brighten. His mouth was open in a silent scream, sure that his own death was seconds away.

The shadow stepped forward, the moonlight striking its face.

Riley smiled at him. "Heya. How ya doing?"

"What...the...fuck?" Brighten asked.

"In a minute. Let's get these explosives in place."

Brighten stared at her, hardly able to understand what had just happened. Moments before he'd been ready to have his bones broken, and now Riley was standing in front of four seemingly dead men.

"Come on. Let's hurry," she whispered.

He took the bag off his shoulder and turned around to look at the castle. He couldn't remember what the hell he was supposed to do. He was trapped in his thoughts.

"It's okay," Riley told him. "Relax. You know what to do."

He closed his eyes, finding his center again. He *did* know what to do.

Brighten got to work, taking the explosives from the bag. They'd detailed the necessary spots at each corner of the hexagon for maximum damage.

Riley helped him once he got the explosives on the ground. Hiding them was the hardest part, but there was plenty of shrubbery around the castle.

Brighten and Riley got them in place, stepping back at the same time to make sure they were well-hidden.

"What do you think?" Riley asked.

Brighten studied his work carefully. Someone *could* detect the explosives, but they'd have to be searching. No one would simply walk up and see what they'd done.

"It'll work, at least for a day or so."

"Okay, I didn't kill these guys because it'd be hard to hide their bodies. We can move them, though, and when they wake up, they won't say anything. They'll be too ashamed and scared," Riley told him, turning away from their handiwork.

They dragged the unconscious sentries away from the explosives. Riley smiled and winked at Brighten.

"Watch this."

She pantsed the guards, leaving them naked and lying next to each other under some trees.

"They definitely won't say a word. Let's get out of here."

The two moved through the castle's garden, Brighten still amazed at what he'd seen. "You were following me?"

"I was watching *you*," she answered.

Brighten had thought that he and Kris knew how to move silently, but he'd never seen anything like Riley could do. The woman moved as if she had no weight, her feet simply gliding over the ground.

"I'm no good to any of you," he told her. "Had you not been there to save my ass, they probably would have beat me to death. I don't even know why I'm involved."

Riley stepped off the path, pulling Brighten with her. She said nothing just then, and neither did Brighten. A moment or so later, two guards walked by.

Brighten had completely missed them. His mind had been so focused on what he was saying that his senses had failed him.

Riley's hadn't, though.

She winked at him and stepped back on the path. "None of what you just said is true. I wasn't following you to make sure you were safe. I was following you to make sure you had the courage."

"Huh?" Brighten heard the words, but he didn't understand.

"I don't need you to be able to fight like me. Only *I* can fight like me. I don't need you to be able to use magic like Worth. Everyone here with me has their own talents. What I needed to make sure was that you had the courage to be here."

They'd reached the edge of the garden and the end of the castle's grounds. A tall wall towered over them.

"Why does courage matter?" Brighten asked.

Riley turned to look at the young man. "Some things matter to me. Loyalty, and you have that. You didn't turn my friends in even though you might have received a reward. I know you're poor, and I know that kind of reward would have been huge for you."

Brighten stared at her for a moment, then looked down. "I never even thought of doing that. Kris didn't either."

"I know." Riley nodded. "The other thing I value is courage. You've done a lot so far, but it's usually when someone is with you. I needed to understand if you could do it on your own. When the chips are down, will you fold or stand firm? You sat there for hours watching those jack-asses, and when you realized you were running out of time, you went forward. You were scared, but you marched up to them anyway, and you did your best. You almost had them leaving, too."

Riley took Brighten's chin and raised it so they were looking each other in the eyes.

"You were brave in the face of overwhelming odds when no one was watching. You could have walked away and told everyone you did what you said you would. We wouldn't have known until it was time to set off the explosives. You didn't. I followed you, and you know what I found out? That you belong with us. I'm glad you're on my side."

Brighten nodded, pride welling in his chest. It was the first time anyone had told him something like that. It was the first time someone had said they wanted him.

He turned to the wall, embarrassed. He hadn't realized which way they were walking, and this thing was entirely too high to get over.

"We've got to find another way," he told her, hoping it would change the subject.

"Nah, we're good," Riley responded.

"How?"

"Are you scared of heights?" Riley asked.

"Why?"

She grinned, her eyes turning red.

Brighten looked down. His feet were no longer touching the ground.

"Remember, Brighten—lean into the fear. See you on the other side."

CHAPTER TEN

K ris looked at her head in the mirror and wanted to scream.

"I can't believe..." Her voice trailed off.

She rubbed her hand over her skull.

There wasn't any hair on it. None.

Worth stood behind her with a razor, long hair around his feet. He was smiling broadly.

Kris whipped around and looked at him. "I hope they string you up when we get there. Hell, I hope they catch me too if it means they get you."

"Not so bad," Worth observed. "Look like me now. Just skinny. No one notice. You look like boy."

Kris shook her head. How long would it take for this shit to grow back? She groaned, not wanting to think about it.

"Holy fuck." Brighten's voice filled the room. "I promise you, Kris, you ain't gonna have to worry about getting a date anytime soon."

Kris looked to her right. Brighten stood in the doorway,

with Riley behind him. Both were smiling. "Say another word and the next date you have is going to be with a doctor, trying to save your balls that I broke."

"It's not so bad," Riley added. "I always keep my hair short. It's easier for fighting."

Kris glared at both of them. "This is ridiculous. I should have never gotten tied up with the likes of any of you."

"Too late." Worth was still grinning. "Time to go. Worth want to be done by happy hour. Wine cheaper."

Kris looked in the mirror again, still hardly able to believe what she was seeing. She had agreed to it, but only because Brighten had come back after finishing his task.

She wasn't going to be outdone by him.

Yet, *he* hadn't had to shave his fucking head.

Kris stood up and looked at her friend. "I'm gonna go do this, but if you say one more word about my head until my hair grows back, you're going to be coughing up blood every time you talk. Understand?"

Brighten grinned but nodded. Kris could tell he was doing his best to keep from laughing.

"Damn it all to hell. Come on, fat man. Let's go see if we can't get ourselves killed."

She stomped out of the room. Worth followed, laughing.

Riley sat in the basement with William, Verith, and Lucie.

Her core group. The ones who represented New Perth.

"Erin and Brighten both dropped off their explosives," Riley confirmed. "Verith, you were able to as well?"

The general nodded.

"And now we're waiting for Worth and Kris. It worries me some, them doing it in broad daylight," Riley told the group.

"If anyone can create confusion enough to hide something on those grounds, it's Worth," William volunteered. "Plus, the girl is a force of nature herself. They're going to be fine."

Riley nodded. "I agree. We need to focus on two things, then: getting Mason before the explosions and setting *off* the explosions."

"What about the people in the castle?" Verith asked.

Riley's eyebrows raised up some. "What do you mean?"

"I hadn't brought it up yet, because war means that innocents die. We're definitely at war, but I figure we should understand what we're doing and be okay with it." Verith grew quiet for a second before continuing, "Not everyone in the castle is guilty. Not everyone serves Rendal. There are a lot of people who are innocent, and when we bring down those walls, they're going to die."

Riley swallowed. She'd been so concerned with how they would save Mason that she hadn't considered anyone else.

"Don't worry, skinny," William commented, clearly seeing her concern. "I know you think you're the only one who can do somethin', but I've been workin' on that."

"You? Working?" Lucie raised one eyebrow. "That seems farfetched."

"Don't you have food to cook or something?" William told her before looking at Riley again. "Kris spread the word to her brother, the one who guards the castle. He's going to let the guards who are loyal to Sidnie know. They're spreading it through the castle; all they need to know is go time. They'll be cleared out."

William turned back to Lucie.

"See, old woman, that's called usin' your brain."

"Hell, got to have one to use it," Lucie replied, although it was clear she approved.

"That solves that problem, then," Verith said.

"Kind of. We still need a go time. How are we going to set the damned things off?" Riley asked.

"I'm going to do it," Verith told her.

The room grew gravely still.

William finally spoke. "To hell with that, Verith. None of us are *dying* during this little endeavor."

"No, no," Verith told him. "I've set the charges correctly. They're all placed at very specific spots so that when I light them, the fuses will burn at the correct speed. It'll give me enough time to light them all and get out."

"You're sure?" Riley asked. She didn't want any of her people getting hurt during this.

Verith nodded. "Yes. I did it all purposely. I know where each of them is. I'll light them and be out before anyone knows it's happening."

"Okay, then. The last thing is Mason. That's going to be me, and me alone," Riley told the group.

"What the hell you mean, 'you and you alone?'" William asked. "That's the dumbest shit I've ever heard."

"Oh, is it?" Riley grinned. "Because you calling Erin 'my lady' all the time seems pretty dumb to me."

"That's got nothin' to do with this," William responded,

his face growing red. "We're talkin' about savin' Mason, and you ain't doin' it alone."

"She has to," Lucie said.

William looked at the older woman. "Why are you here? Go cook somethin'!"

"Talk to me like that again," Lucie responded, "and you'll be the next thing I put in a pot to cook." She calmed a bit. "Riley has to do it alone because everything has to happen at the same time."

William's eyes narrowed. "Go on."

"If we go get Mason now, Rendal's going to know. The walls have to fall at nearly the exact time she's grabbing Mason. It's the only way to create enough confusion that the bastard doesn't know what's happening."

"So? That don't mean she has to do it alone. She's still going to need help," William shot back.

Lucie sighed, shaking her head. She looked at Riley, a slight grin pulling at her mouth. "Strong, but he's never gonna be bright, is he?" She turned to Verith. "Tell him what's going to happen when the castle comes down."

"Debris and rock are going to fly forth at deadly speeds," the general said. "The castle walls will keep them from going *too* far, so the populace is going to be safe. The square won't be, though. It's too close, and the destruction is going to make it out there."

"I don't give a damn." William wasn't going to give up. "I'll outrun the rocks and whatever else is there. Riley isn't going to get Mason alone."

"You're not *understanding*," Lucie stressed. "You can't outrun that much force. It's too fast. That's why she has to go alone. She'll be able to protect herself and Mason, and she'll be able to get them out of there quickly. But anyone else she has to protect is going to create more risk. You being there will make it harder for her to save Mason and herself."

William opened his mouth to say something, but no words came out.

After a second, he turned to Riley. "I don't like it."

"Don't matter." Riley smiled. "That's the way it will be. I'll get him and bring him back here, and then we're home free. We'll all go back to New Perth."

"What about Rendal?" Lucie asked. "How do we make sure he dies?"

"He'll be in the castle," Verith volunteered. "No way he lives. I don't care how strong his magic is, he can't hold back thousands of pounds of stone."

Lucie nodded, although Riley didn't think she looked completely convinced.

"What is it, Lucie?" Riley asked.

"I just don't like not being able to confirm that the bastard is dead." She shook her head. "I don't trust him, and when we leave here, I want this over."

"I understand," Verith said, "but he'll be dead. He's not going to survive. None of them will. The weapons, his scientist—all of them are going to be destroyed."

"Okay." Lucie sighed. "I guess you're right."

"He is," Riley said. "All right, when is go time? We need to make sure the people in the castle understand when they have to be out by."

"Once again, I've taken care of a lot of this," William told them. "My brain is clearly working at a much higher capacity than anyone else's. *Especially* yours, Lucie. The best time is going to be the morning shift change. The people getting off can actually *leave*, and those supposed to come in will just stay at home. It'll be the easiest."

Riley looked at Verith. "That will work?"

He nodded. "Yeah. As soon as Worth gets back, we'll know we're ready. We can send the word out then."

"Okay." Riley stood. She felt good about it. Everything was as it should be, and for once Rendal wasn't one step ahead. "We're going to win. We're going to finally kick his fucking ass."

Everyone around the table nodded.

When William spoke, he was grinning. "You'd think a lady of her stature would use better language."

CHAPTER ELEVEN

"Artino said that he thought there was a break-in down in his laboratory." Harold stood on the balcony, behind Rendal.

The mage stared at the cage in the kingdom's square. Rendal could see it from here, although not in detail. Of course, he could send his mind down there and understand it better, but there wasn't any need for that at the moment.

"Is that what he's calling it? The bowels of the castle are his *laboratory*?" Rendal asked.

"Yes, sir," Harold answered.

"The man continually makes me laugh." He didn't turn away as he spoke. This didn't concern him much. Mason was all that mattered right now, because Riley would come for him sooner or later. She wouldn't be able to help herself. "Tell me what happened."

"The guards we put down there were attacked."

"Have you spoken with them?" Rendal asked.

"I did—"

"Hold on," the mage interrupted. "They only told *Artino* they'd been attacked?"

"Yes, sir. They were embarrassed. They said it was a woman who did it."

Rendal whipped around, anger seizing him.

"Sir, I've checked with all of them," Harold continued calmly. "It wasn't the Right Hand. This woman had red hair, and while lethal, she wasn't as deadly as Riley."

Rendal felt his rage subsiding. Some, at least. "But these imbeciles didn't tell anyone?"

"No, sir, but I've dealt with it. That won't be a problem again."

Rendal nodded. "Thank you, Harold. My apologies. This has been a stressful few days." He turned back around to stare at the cage. "Continue. What did these morons tell you?"

"Well, pretty much that this woman showed up and kicked their asses, and that's all they remember," Harold started. "I performed an investigation within those working inside the laboratory. From what I can tell, no one saw that woman or anything out of the ordinary."

"So we know these guards got their asses kicked but nothing else?" Rendal asked.

"Yes, sir. My opinion is that we have bigger things to deal with. If someone got down there to the laboratory, there is nothing we can do right now. Focusing on finding the redhaired woman will take attention away from finding the Right Hand."

Rendal nodded. "I agree, Harold. Hell, it could have been one of the guard's mistresses, pissed off, and they just don't want to admit it. Just make sure the men are punished severely for not reporting it."

"Yes, sir. That's already been handled," Harold answered.

"Have you heard or seen anything else about Riley?" She was all Rendal gave a damn about. The Right Hand.

"There was a report of something abnormal last evening, but we can't confirm it was the Right Hand or one of her minions," Harold responded.

"Yes, yes. I heard about the ice. I'm not concerned." Rendal turned around and looked at Harold. Rendal was tired, and his bracelet was empty. It'd been empty for hours. He would be teaching his class soon, and he would have to refill the bracelet first.

He stepped toward Harold. "I can't be everywhere at once, but I feel like I have to be right now. This operation...*your* operation, it's too haphazard. There are too many moving pieces, and I don't think you have control of it, Harold. How many men are beneath you?"

"Including Sidnie's men?"

Rendal nodded.

"Two thousand. Maybe more."

"Exactly," Rendal answered. "You don't even know. This place is a mess, and the more I talk to you, the messier I think it is. I'm *exhausting* myself, Harold. I'm having to send my mind out almost constantly looking for this woman when we should already have her."

Harold swallowed but said nothing.

Rendal worked to keep his anger in check. He knew that lashing out too harshly right now would hurt his overall goal.

"Something is... Something is growing, Harold," the mage continued as he stared at his second-in-command. "Something is about to happen. I can feel it. I'm standing out here watching this cage, but for the first time, I'm not in control, Harold. I don't know where she is. I can't bring her to me. Do you understand?"

"What do you need me to do?" Harold asked. "Just tell me, and I'll do it."

"Find her," Rendal whispered. "Find her and bring her to me."

Harold nodded. "I won't quit until it's accomplished."

"If it's not accomplished soon, you won't have to quit," the mage told him. "Because I'm going to quit *you*, Harold. Now get out of my sight, and don't return until you have actionable information. Don't return until you can tell me where the hell she is."

"Yes, sir," Harold responded. He turned from the balcony and walked back inside, leaving Rendal to himself.

The mage went back to staring at the cage.

He wasn't lying to Harold. Something was amiss, but he couldn't understand what. They were still terrorizing the citizenry, pulling people out of their houses day and night, but that hadn't brought Riley to him.

Now her Assistant Prefect hung in the middle of the kingdom, his body being drained of nanocytes.

And she *still* hadn't come to him.

Rendal couldn't find her, regardless of what he did.

Why?

There was no one to lash out at, either. Sidnie's damn Prefect was the only one, but he was basically brain-dead. He stood in the tower drooling on himself all day long.

Focus, the mage told himself. *Don't get lost in your thoughts. Find her.*

Rendal turned away from the balcony and walked back into the tower. He closed the door to the balcony and made his way to the couch.

Someone had discovered Artino's laboratory. Perhaps he had dismissed that too quickly. Harold's operation was like herding damn cats right now, and just because Harold hadn't discovered what happened didn't mean Rendal couldn't.

If someone had gotten down there, they'd know what Rendal was building.

They'd know about the weapons.

Rendal didn't close his eyes as he folded his legs beneath him.

Instead, he left them open while they flared red. The dark mage stared forward, his tired mind beginning to search again for the woman he desperately wanted.

Kris didn't know if Worth was drunk or just pretending to be. She was beginning to wonder if *he* even knew.

His lips and mouth were purple, but that could be a permanent condition for the bald man.

Yet, somehow, they had made their way through the castle's gates.

The guards didn't know what to do with the bald drunk who claimed to have important business in the castle. Every time Kris thought a guard was going to crack his skull open with a club, another door opened for them.

At the moment, they were walking down a long cobblestone path toward the castle's main doors.

Worth, wearing his goofy grin, looked down at Kris and winked at her. He had a canteen full of wine in his right hand, and he regularly brought it up to his mouth to drink.

Kris said nothing.

The deeper they moved into the castle, the less she wanted to be here. No one had noticed her yet, partly because Worth had said she was a boy and his protege and partly because her fucking head was bald.

Kris just wanted out of here. She'd seen that damn mage and his underling and been far too close to death to be fucking around inside here.

Yet Worth had said he needed her.

That was why she was here—because he said in his broken language that he couldn't do it without her.

The man showed no fear at all, while she felt more like Brighten with each step.

They reached the castle's main door. It was massive, meant to indicate the riches inside the building.

The guard who had led the two of them here stopped in front of his superior.

Kris and Worth stood about ten feet away, farther down the stairs that led to the door.

"That guy, the bald one, says they have business with the Economic Minister." The guard sneered as he spoke, glancing down at Worth. Kris wanted to fold into herself.

"With the Economic Minister?" the superior asked. "This man here?"

He took a few steps toward them, ignoring the other guard. "What business do you have? The Economic

Minister doesn't have time for merchants off the street, and you look like a fuckin' drunk anyway." He turned back to the guard who led them here. "Why the hell did you bring them to me? The man's mouth is purple because he's been drinkin' all damn day!"

The guard looked confused, like he couldn't remember why he'd brought them here.

The drunk bastard is using magic, Kris thought. She hadn't been staring at Worth the whole time so she didn't know if his eyes had turned red, but... Well, it made no sense that they'd gotten this far, and that guard couldn't give a good reason for it either.

"Answer me, man!" the superior yelled.

The underling looked at Worth. "Tell him what you told me. Tell him your business now, or I swear I'm going to beat you so hard the rest of your body will be the same color as your mouth!"

Kris wanted to bolt. She talked a lot of shit, and she could back up a lot, too, but this was getting absurd. They were inside the castle's walls, and now about to be inside the castle, yet they needed to get to one of the corners on the outside.

And now the guards were threatening to beat the hell out of them.

Kris's face remained unchanged, showing nothing of the fear rolling through her.

"Worth tell you already," the bald man scolded. "Have important information regarding pig health. *Dangerous* information."

"Pig health?" The superior was incredulous. "You think you're going to get inside the castle to speak with the

Economic Minister over pig health?" Again he looked at the first guard. "You're out of your damn mind, bringing him to me over nothing."

Kris was staring at Worth now, and for the first time, she saw that his eyes were red. He was using magic, although she had no idea what he was doing.

"Your mother concerned with pig health," Worth told them. "She pig-fucker."

Kris was starting to understand.

He'd gotten this far, and now he was going to royally piss them off.

He's either insane or a genius, she thought.

"What the fuck did you say?" The head guard turned to him. Worth's eyes were still red, but Kris didn't know if the guard could see it.

"Said your mother fuck pigs. She want know if there health issues."

They were making sense now, his plans, and Kris held a certain respect for him. The bald man was about to catch a beating, but it would give her an excuse to run.

Right to the place she needed to be.

Worth's eyes returned to their normal color. Kris still didn't know for sure what he'd been doing, but from the looks of things, he'd been making the guards angrier.

"Welp," the superior said, "looks like you want an ass-beating, and I'm just the man to do it."

He unsheathed his club.

Worth looked at Kris and winked, then stared back at the two guards. "Worth look out for your mother. Why you mad?"

The guard swung his club, and Worth brought his arm up to block it.

Kris knew what to do. She wanted to help, to try to stop the ass-beating Worth was surely going to receive, but that wasn't why he'd brought her. She had moves to make, and his sacrifice here was going to allow her to do it.

She turned and ran.

Kris looked over her shoulder only briefly. The second guard had joined the first, forgetting about the kid that the bald man had come with. He was going to have fun beating the hell out of that smart-mouthed merchant.

Kris turned back to the path in front of her.

Do your part, she thought. *Make sure that beating he's taking is worth it.*

CHAPTER TWELVE

"Holy fuck, man," William admonished. "What the hell happened to you?"

Riley's stomach rose into her throat as she looked at Worth.

William turned on Kris. "How the hell did this happen? Where the hell were you?"

Worth struggled into the room and practically fell into the first chair he saw.

His right eye had swollen shut, badly bruised to a deep purple. His lips—usually purple—were now split and red. Welts and more bruises covered his arms and legs. His usually tan skull was scraped nearly raw.

"Not her fault," Worth managed to say. "She do fine."

He slumped in the chair.

"Get him some water," Riley commanded.

Lucie scampered from the room without another word.

"What happened?" Riley whispered.

Worth pointed to Kris, clearly not having the energy to give answers.

"I'm sorry," Kris told the room. For the first time, the girl looked lost. "I had no idea it would be this bad."

"Worth okay," he assured everyone. A string of blood dripped from his lips to his chin.

"It's fine." Riley moved toward the girl, still standing at the room's entrance. She put her arm around Kris and directed her to a chair.

Kris sat as Lucie entered the room, bringing two glasses of water.

She handed the first one to Worth and brought the other to Kris.

Worth drank greedily, then put the glass on the table. "No more water. Bring wine. Lots of wine."

"Father save me," Lucie murmured. She said nothing else though, only left the room to go find the alcohol.

Riley turned to Kris. "What happened?"

"I didn't know it would be like this." Kris stared at Worth as if she couldn't believe it.

"Hey." Riley squatted in front of her chair and placed a hand on her leg. "Hey, it's okay. We just need to know what happened. No one is blaming you. Not William, not me, not anyone. Just talk to us, because Worth can't right now."

Kris swallowed and tried to meet Riley's eyes. "We followed his plan. He got us inside the castle walls and up to the main entrance. I think he must have been using magic."

She looked at Worth, and he nodded in agreement.

"Wine!" Worth hollered into the kitchen.

"Hold your damned horses!" Lucie shouted back.

Riley ignored them, turning back to Kris. "Keep going."

"When we got to the entrance, he started talking shit to

the guards. Before we got there, I mean, I was carrying the explosives. He didn't have anything on him, and I thought it was just because he was scared." Kris shook her head. "When he started talking shit, the guards didn't waste any time. They lit into him. I didn't have a choice; I had to run. That's the whole reason I was holding the explosives, right, Worth?"

She glanced at the bald man. He nodded but quickly turned his attention to Lucie, who was walking into the room holding a jug of wine.

"Here, ya drunk. I hope ya gag on it," Lucie murmured, although she was smiling slightly.

Worth took the jug, his usual grin on his face now.

"He definitely has a one-track mind," William commented.

Riley redirected her attention to Kris. "Okay, that makes sense. You didn't do anything wrong. Worth made the decision to get you in that way, and you followed his lead." She looked at Worth. "He's going to be okay, aren't ya, Worth?"

The big man nodded, putting the jug down for a second. "Worth fine. You worry too much."

"Now, Kris," Riley continued. "Did you set the explosives? Are they where they need to be? Worth might look bad right now, but nothing is broken. Understand, with his magic, he could have easily wiped those guards out. But he didn't because they couldn't know his real intentions. The important thing here is, did you get the job done?"

Kris nodded. She wiped her eyes, brushing tears away. "They're all in place. I hid them, too. You can't see them. All we have to do is light the fuses."

Riley nodded, placing both hands on the girl's shoulders. "Good. That is good, good news. That's what is most important. Worth will be just fine."

"Just fine," Worth agreed.

Verith walked into the room, halting as soon as he laid eyes on Worth. "*This* was your plan?"

"Shut up." Worth grinned and turned the jug up again.

Verith only shook his head. "Did we at least complete the mission? Are all the explosives in place?"

Riley nodded. "They're in place. We're ready to bring the whole damned thing to the ground."

"Okay." Verith looked at William. "Let's go ahead and get the word out. Tomorrow morning at dawn, that castle is falling. Anyone innocent needs to be far away."

William turned to Kris. "All right, kid. We got another job to do. You up to it?"

Kris nodded although her eyes were still full of tears.

"Trust me, kid. Worth ain't easy to break. His head is full of rocks, so nothing inside can even be damaged, ya understand?" William winked at the girl. "Now, let's go spread the word that the mage who did it to him is about to die. Sound good?"

Kris nodded again, wiping her eyes a final time. She stood up and looked at Worth. "I'm sorry."

"Hush!" Worth practically shouted. "Worth fine! You women worry too much! Go! Go! Leave Worth drink in peace!"

Kris laughed at the man's frustration. "You're a real dick, Worth."

"Big dick, yes." Worth nodded, grinning wildly. "Now go! Leave Worth in peace!"

The moon was high outside, the day's work completed. It was past midnight, and Riley sat with William and Verith.

"Everything is ready? You were able to get the word out to everyone?" she asked William.

"Yeah. It wasn't a problem. The castle's staff is already terrified, so they're looking for any reason to believe. I spoke to Erin and she spread the word among the military, at least those who aren't gung-ho about killing New Perth." He shrugged. "The ones who want to go to war with us will probably die, but there's going to be casualties."

Riley didn't like it, but she couldn't do anything about it. She turned to Verith. "And you—you're ready to do your part?"

"Of course," he answered.

"You're going to make it out alive, right?"

Verith nodded. "Without a doubt. Everything is set up so I just have to light the fuses and keep moving. Nothing to it. I'll be out of the destruction's path."

Riley nodded, then turned to William. "You know your job?"

"Yeah, I know my job. Make sure everyone we brought here is ready to go outside Sidnie's walls."

"Simple job for a simple man." She grinned.

"Hell, I'd go get Mason myself if you weren't trying to hog all the glory. I'd go blow the damn castle up, too. I'm basically giving you guys some glory because I've been taking it all since this whole thing started." William looked up at the ceiling, a smile crossing his face. "I've been thinking a lot about what I want my statue to look like when

I return. You know, whether it should be marble or maybe even gold? Should I be flexing in it? So many questions."

"All right, be quiet," Riley told him good-naturedly. "Verith, I need to know the signal for when to grab Mason. How will I know when the explosions are about to go off?"

Verith smiled. "That's something else I've set up. Right before it explodes, you're going to see tiny explosions shooting into the sky. When you see them, get to work freeing Mason. The explosions will happen a few minutes after that."

Riley nodded. "And how bad is the rubble going to be?"

Verith sighed. "That's the tough part. The walls will hold some back, but it's still going to be bad. You'll have to guard yourself and Mason well."

Riley stood up. That was what she had figured, and she was fine with it. She just needed to hear it from Verith. "Okay, gentlemen—and William—let's go finish this."

"I take issue with your characterization of me as anything less than a gentleman," William responded. "For such an affront, I'm going to ensure that as part of my monument, you will bow in front of me forever. The Prefect will approve it, of course."

Riley rolled her eyes. "Just make sure the people here are safe, chubby."

"And you make sure Mason is safe, skinny." William winked at her.

"How is he doing?" Rendal asked Harold.

"Mason?"

"Yes," the mage answered. He was still sitting on the couch staring forward. His eyes blazed red.

"He's weakening, but he's stronger than most from what I can tell. I left him about an hour ago," Harold told his master.

"How much time does he have left, do you think? Before we drain too much of him?"

"Four days at this pace. Maybe five."

Rendal didn't nod or move. He just kept staring.

Harold remained standing at the side of the couch. "Is there anything else you need of me, sir?"

"Still no word from Riley?"

"No, sir," Harold responded.

"He will not need to last four days," Rendal whispered. "They're going to do something soon. Perhaps tonight, or perhaps tomorrow during the day."

Harold didn't dare question the mage.

"Have your men check every nook and cranny of the premises. I want every single stone of this building checked. Do you understand?" Rendal asked.

"Yes, sir. I'll start it immediately."

"I'm going down to Mason. If they're going to attempt something, it'll include freeing him. She'll be the one to do that. When she does, I'll be waiting for her."

"That seems wise, sir," Harold agreed. "Would you like me to begin the inspection?"

The mage nodded. The fire in his eyes died, and he looked at his second-in-command. "What time is it?"

"Three in the morning, sir."

Rendal had canceled his classes earlier, intent on discovering Riley's plans.

"Yes, begin the inspections. Harold, you need to be prepared. Something is going to happen very soon. I can't see everything. Truthfully, I can't see much. Lucie and that other man are blocking a lot of my sight, but I can tell they're planning something."

Rendal looked forward, nodding to himself.

"Exactly as I thought they would. They can't handle leaving their Assistant Prefect dying in public like that, so they'll come tonight, or tomorrow. Either way, be prepared."

His eyes flashed to Harold. "I fear, old friend, that if you're not prepared, you may die. I fear that we all may."

Riley remained hidden. She was alone for the first time in a long time. For weeks, she'd constantly been with someone—Worth, William. Even those bastards Belarus and Harold.

Now, though, she was alone and watching Mason. The moon was nearly below the horizon, and the sun would be rising soon. Two people would determine what happened next: Verith and her. Perhaps Verith was the most important because she was depending on him to move toward Mason.

Part of her wished she had waited with Alexandra and the Chosen. That she had learned more, especially Psychic Magic. She wished she could reach forth and talk to Mason, who hung in the cage. She couldn't, though.

She had to simply wait, and when the explosives sprang into the sky, *move*.

Time was growing short.

This would all be over soon.

Verith hadn't counted how many men he'd had to kill to get inside the castle's walls. The number was growing higher, but he still hadn't arrived at where he needed to be.

The men he killed weren't good guys. He was certain of that because the good guys had already left or weren't showing up for work. The ones still here were loyal to the mage, so their deaths meant nothing to Verith.

He'd reached the first of the six corners.

He stood in the darkness, looking out at the area. He had to do this quickly, but he also didn't want to be reckless. There was always a chance that they'd been discovered and he was walking into a trap.

Verith saw no one.

He stepped out of the darkness, pulling the matches from his pocket. This set of explosives had the longest fuse. If his math was correct—which he really fucking hoped it was—he would be able to move from corner to corner of the castle to light them all, and when he finished, run out before they all blew at the same time.

If his math was off... Well, Verith would be blowing up with the rest of the castle.

Verith approached the castle wall, still unable to see the explosives. This corner was Erin's; she'd done an excellent job of hiding the bombs.

Verith reached the corner and squatted, looking behind the large bush.

There it is, he thought. *Good job, Erin. Good fucking job.*

He brought the matches up to his eyes, ready to light them.

"It really was a genius idea."

Verith turned, standing up in one smooth motion that rivaled Riley's speed.

"Whose idea was it?"

Verith knew the man standing in front of him—or knew *of* him at least. The mage's second-in-command, Harold.

"Mine," Verith told him. He held the matches at his side now, no longer even thinking about lighting them.

Harold stood seven feet away with ten guards behind him. They were all heavily armored and armed. Harold had his sword already drawn.

"I mean, it really was a smart idea. I've finally put it all together," the head guard said. "I can't say I did it by myself, of course. Rendal was the one who put me on the correct course. The man is more powerful than any of you can imagine, and that's where your fault lies. You keep thinking you can beat him, but you can't."

Harold smiled, a sad thing that spoke only of pity for Verith and his friends.

"You see, Rendal saw that something was about to happen. He didn't know what, but his instructions are always spot on. He told me to inspect every stone of the castle, so I did. I started four hours ago, and I found your explosives. That was when I put it together."

Harold gestured toward them.

"They're at every critical structural position of the castle, and there's enough to level it. The entire damned building. I understood then. You guys saw what we've got downstairs, didn't you?"

Verith nodded. There wasn't any sense in lying now. He was caught, and while there was a chance he might fight his way out, it was small.

"And rather than try to go down there and destroy it all and then fight your way out, you decided to just bring the whole thing down at once?"

Verith nodded again.

Harold smiled. "Truly a genius plan. You would have pulled it off, killing us all in one swoop. You have my respect."

"Keep your fucking respect." Verith gritted his teeth. He knew it was nearly time.

"I will, then. I have to tell you that I can't let you light those explosives, though. In fact, I can't let you leave this place."

"You can try to stop me," Verith responded. He unsheathed his sword. "You see the blood on it? That's from those who tried to stop me from getting in here."

Harold looked at the wet blood on the steel. "Ah, yes. You were racking up quite a body count. I'm sort of sorry to see it end, but..." He shrugged. "What can you do?"

Verith raised his sword.

"One question before we begin this dance," Harold interrupted. "There has to be some signal. I imagine—as does Rendal—that you're going to be attempting to break Mason out of his prison at the same time you blow this place to hell. What's the signal?"

"The signal is when my friends hear you screaming," Verith said. "Then they'll know that it's time to get to work."

"Not going to make this easy on me, huh?" Harold asked.

Verith moved forward, his sword at the ready.

The sound of his steel echoed in the early morning.

He fought admirably, but in the end, there were simply too many enemies.

When the sun rose, Riley knew something was wrong. It'd broken over the horizon ten minutes before, and still she'd seen no explosions shooting into the sky.

Mason was finally waking in his cage. He looked worse than ever.

Riley remained atop the building, staring at him, her body ready for war but the sign not coming.

What is wrong? she wondered.

Nothing. It's just taking longer than expected.

She told herself that, but she didn't believe it.

Something was off.

"RILEY!" The voice echoed off the buildings surrounding the square. "ENOUGH WITH THE CHARADE! COME DOWN! YOUR PLOT HAS BEEN FOILED! IT'S OVER!"

She knew that voice. There wasn't any doubt in her mind. *Rendal.*

She stood, able to see a bit more of the square.

The mage stood in the middle.

He wore his robe, the hood off, revealing himself to the world. His face immediately turned to her when she stood up.

There you are, his voice filled her head. *Come down and let's talk. There are no explosions coming.*

His eyes were bright red.

Riley unsheathed her sword and stepped to the edge of the building. Her own eyes lit red and she stepped off the side, slowly floating to the ground. She landed softly, her eyes returning to normal.

"Where's Verith?" Her voice was steel moving across ice.

"He's dead, Riley. I told you back on my ship that I'd take everything from you, and so I am. Your Prefect's top general is dead, his blood staining the grounds of Sidnie's castle."

Riley smiled. "You're lying."

"If I am, then where are the explosions? Why isn't wind carrying rocks and screams right now? Why is the castle still standing behind me?" The mage smiled. "I'm not lying, Riley, and you know it."

She glanced up at Mason. He was standing in the cage, his hands gripping the bars closest to her. He shook his head but remained silent. She knew what he was saying: *No. Don't fight him. Escape.*

Fuck that, she thought.

She looked back at Rendal. "I guess this means you're ready to die, coming out here all alone."

He smiled. "You've learned some magic, I see. I could tell the moment you entered the kingdom. You and I— we're meant to be."

"We're meant to be like water and fire are meant to be, you psychopath."

Rendal continued as if he hadn't heard her. "I wanted you to come to me when you first got here because you don't understand what's coming out of you. You don't understand your magic or your potential. I didn't want to be forced to kill you, which I might have been if I hadn't acted."

"Kill me?" Riley almost laughed. "You've faced me time and time again, but you've never been able to hurt me no matter how hard you tried."

"Because I want you *alive*, Riley. Not dead. But had you been successful in detonating those bombs or destroying my weapons, I would have been forced to take action. I don't have to now. You and I, we can still rule together."

"You're delusional. Truly, Rendal." Riley shook her head, unable to believe the man. "You are delusional on a level I can hardly understand. I'm taking Mason, but I *will* grant you quarter. If you let me and my friends leave, I will not chase you anymore. If you keep away from my kingdom and from those I care about, I won't kill you."

The mage smiled. "Do you think you have control here? Is that what all this is? The castle still stands, your general dead at my guards' feet? Your Assistant Prefect hanging in a cage behind me, his body being drained of its very *life*. Does that make you think you're in charge?"

"Stand in my way at your peril," she told the mage.

Riley started walking forward, her eyes turning red. She was only concerned with getting Mason. Freeing him from the cage and returning to New Perth.

The mage began to laugh.

Riley didn't look at him as she approached the cage.

She reached it, standing beneath the metal bars. Mason was looking down at her.

She reached into the air, focusing on the bars trapping Mason.

Riley blinked, and when she opened her eyes, the mage was standing inside the cage. He was behind Mason, his hand wrapped around the Assistant Prefect's throat, his eyes red. "You or him, Riley. Right now. Choose."

She stared upward.

"You pledge allegiance to me now or he dies. It's as simple as that. Your honor will hold you to me." Rendal nodded. "Your life for his."

"No, Riley," Mason told her, his voice strained. "It'll never end. If you pledge yourself to him, he'll still come for New Perth. He'll never stop. I command you not to do this."

Riley took two steps back, her eyes not fading from red nor looking anywhere but into Rendal's cruel eyes.

"Quickly, Riley, or I kill him," the mage commanded.

Her senses took in everything around her. Her body was poised to act, a fighting machine once again. Now, though, she added magic to the mix.

And the death of a friend.

Verith was dead, and he hadn't deserved that. He'd been trying to *help*.

And this sonofa-fucking-bitch had Mason, his hand wrapped around the Assistant Prefect's neck.

"Oh, I can see your wheels turning, Riley," the mage spat. "You're an open book to me. Even now, your mind is deciding on war. You think you can kill me. That you can beat me back. He will die, and you will still join. Bow. Take my hand. Kiss my bracelet. He can live, and we can rule together."

Riley's eyes narrowed.

For a single second, she considered it. Letting Mason out of that cage and taking his place, only instead of having a hand wrapped around her neck, she would be on her knees, head bowed to the insane monster inside.

"No," she whispered. "No. We will both die before we serve you."

Mason nodded. "Yes, that's right. Death before dishonor."

A sick smile spread across Rendal's face. "So be it."

His hand erupted into flames only seconds before hers did.

She raised them to the sky, blasting streaks of fire from them.

The flames slammed into the cage, melting the bars even as fire raced across Mason's throat.

She bent her knees slightly, unsheathing her sword and placing the point on the ground. She leapt into the air, kicking toward the burning cage. The weakened metal bent beneath her strength and she pushed herself inside.

Her right hand flashed out, grabbing Mason's wrist. She flung him *hard,* wrenching him free of the dark mage. He flew across the cage, slamming into the bars. His body was on fire, but he was alive.

Riley turned away from Mason, trusting him to handle himself. She looked at Rendal. "You missed your chance, and now you're fucked."

The mage's right hand was still ablaze, and the bracelet

on his wrist was bright green, delivering more nanocytes to his bloodstream.

"Perhaps you must die then," he said. "If you won't bend, I'll break you."

Rendal tossed his left hand up and Riley flew across the cage, unable to stop herself. She hit the opposite side, her head colliding with the metal.

Riley saw stars as she turned to face her enemy.

Flames raced toward her, Rendal turning the cage into a fiery hell.

Riley brought her hands together, her own flames slashing out. They hit Rendal's, stopping his attack.

She bared her teeth, set her feet, and forced more flames out of her hands.

The heat grew tremendously, sweat pouring down her face. The fire in front of her partially hid the mage, yet his powerful flames continued pressing against her own.

He's too strong, she thought. *I can't beat him by force of will.*

Riley spun, her fire dying as Rendal's slammed into the place she had just been. The cage shuddered, the metal bending and then breaking as flames rushed into the morning sky.

Riley quickly spun around the pole in the middle, coming at Rendal's side, her sword flashing. She swung it down hard toward his collarbone.

The mage turned his head, staring at her with his bright red eyes.

A blue shield shot up from his shoulders. It looked ephemeral, but when Riley's sword slammed into it, sparks flew upward.

She wasted no time, but simply brought the sword low, swiping it at his Achilles tendons. The mage jumped over the attack as if it were a child's game of jump rope.

He brought his hand up, his speed rivaling hers, and smashed it into her nose.

Blood splattered across Riley's face as she backed up. Her vision blurred as hot tears rushed to her eyes.

The mage turned, flames burning across the metal cage. Everything was hot. Riley could feel the bottom of the cage burning through her boots.

"Ready to die?" Rendal asked.

Riley looked down at her feet.

Worth had told her she wasn't ready.

William had told her she should wait.

Yet, she'd come anyway, and now here she was, in front of the monster she'd been chasing for so long. Only, she wasn't strong enough. She wasn't powerful enough to stop him.

"Yes, that's right," Rendal agreed. "Your potential is great, but you understand nothing. You're like a child in a world you don't know. I was to be the one to show you the way, but you ruined all that and now you'll die. Then your precious Mason will die. Then your precious *kingdom* will die. Know that, silly girl. Everything you love will still fall, but unfortunately, you'll be too dead to notice."

He smiled.

Maybe Worth had been right. Maybe she *should* have stayed with the Chosen. Maybe she'd made mistake after mistake to end up in this inferno, facing a man who seemed to know no bounds.

But she was here all the same.

And she was a fucking Right Hand.

She had trained for many years to fight for Justice and defend the kingdom at all costs, even if it cost her life.

And if that was what this took, her life, then so-fuck-ing-be-it.

Riley looked up. "Let's see if you got what it takes to kill me, old man."

She rushed forward, eyes blazing red and sword slashing. She swung the blade with her right hand, streaming both lightning and flames from her left.

The mage parried with his magic, both dodging and meeting her attacks.

Riley didn't stop moving forward, slamming her sword down repeatedly, the mage giving ground as the fire grew around them. It reached out for her, singeing Riley's skin. She kept forcing herself forward, battering the mage backward.

Finally, she had his back against the burning bars. He wore a smile even as he defended against her attacks, his hands moving as fast as hers, having backed up as far as possible.

Riley focused on her sword, seeing its beautiful metal in her mind.

A blue shield wrapped around the mage but Riley hardly noticed.

She brought her sword down a final time, all her energy and force focusing solely on killing this man.

It hit the blue shield, flames ripping forth from her steel as electricity filled the air around them.

Riley barely saw the explosion.

One moment she was trying to slice through Rendal's

shield and the next she was flying into the air, the bars that had held her firm shattered. Higher and higher she went, frantically searching for Mason.

An explosion ripped forth, a combination of fire, wind, and electricity. It broke the cobblestones beneath and cracked the castle's walls. It crumbled and burnt the buildings surrounding the square, everything engulfed in a fiery blaze.

Riley hit the ground hard, bouncing on her back before skidding to a stop.

Her eyes were closed, her breathing shallow.

Moments passed as the world burnt around her.

And then her brain forced her body up. She rose to her feet, her eyes flashing open. Her body ached, and her skin was singed. She saw only fire and smoke around her, yet Mason had to be *somewhere*.

"MASON!" she shouted, not caring if Rendal heard her. Not caring if he was hunting for her in this hell. "*MASON!*"

She rushed forward. The heat and flames tried to kill her, but she kept going. Her eyes watered and her body hurt, yet she had to find him.

"Riley..."

It was a soft whisper, nearly drowned by the sound of flames engulfing the world.

She turned in the direction it came from.

"Riley..." It was Mason.

She ran over, finding him crumpled on the ground. His arm was bent in a way it shouldn't be, as was his leg. His body was badly burnt, his neck a painful mix of black and red flesh.

"Come on." She reached down, grabbing him gently under his arms.

"No. You've got to run," he told her. "You're not going to make it carrying me."

Riley shook her head, grabbing her leader and lifting him. "You're as dumb as William if you think I'm leaving you, Mason. I didn't burn this kingdom to the ground just to let you burn with it."

Her muscles cried out as she started walking, the Assistant Prefect in her arms.

"You won't make it." He started coughing, the smoke filling both their lungs.

"We're both going to make it, now shut up, Mason."

Riley went forward, step after step. She saw no one. Heard no one. She had to turn back from certain pathways, the fire too hot.

The world began to grow hazy, but not from smoke. Mason had passed out in her arms, and Riley felt her knees start to buckle.

Forward, she thought. *Keep going forward.*

She went another ten feet and then fell to the ground. Blackness overtook the Right Hand.

CHAPTER THIRTEEN

"She's too stubborn to die."

Riley heard the words, the first she could remember hearing in... Well, what seemed like *forever*.

She opened her eyes.

"Told you. *Way* too stubborn to die."

It was William, and he was looking down at her.

"Mason?" she asked, her vocal cords feeling like someone was rubbing sandpaper over them.

"Quiet, my Savior," Thomas said. "Quiet now. You need rest."

"The bastard is still going on about you being his savior." William chuckled.

Riley reached out, unsure where she was or what was happening. She gripped William's arm as tight as she could. "Mason?" It was the only word she could get out.

"Calm down, skinny. He's alive. Hurt, but he's gonna make it. Now listen to your little lackey here and get some sleep."

Riley stared at William for a moment, searching for any sense of falsehood in his face.

She saw none. He was telling the truth. Wherever she was right now, whatever was happening, Mason was alive.

She closed her eyes, and yet again, darkness overtook the Right Hand.

William hated being underground. To him, the entire place felt too small, like he was trapped.

Probably because he was a damned giant.

Yet, right now they had no choice. He'd spoken to Riley briefly, but they couldn't move her any farther. Making it this far across the desert had been hard enough. Going all the way to New Perth in such a state?

She would have died, as would Mason.

They'd been here five days, and while William talked bullishly, he didn't feel that way. Not about Riley, at least.

Mason was already awake. His arm and leg had been set, and while he wouldn't be walking on his own anytime soon, the Assistant Prefect was doing well.

Riley was not.

William and Mason had been summoned to the queen's chambers. Her name was Alexandra, and while William knew she was only the queen of a few underground tunnels, he was beginning to trust her.

Everyone in here had an almost slavish devotion to Riley.

They truly believed her to be some kind of savior; they believed her magic would grow that powerful.

William didn't know about all that, only that his friend was sick and not getting better.

Mason was in a type of chair William hadn't seen back in New Perth. The thing had wheels on the sides and William was pushing it from behind, ensuring that Mason could get wherever he needed.

"How are you feeling, sir?" he asked the Assistant Prefect.

"Please cut that shit out, William," Mason directed. "I feel awful, but there's no reason for us to continue with the sirs and such, given how far you've come for me. We're friends."

"Yes, sir," William responded before snapping his teeth shut. It didn't matter what Mason wanted; he wouldn't be able to stop etiquette.

They reached the queen's chambers. William stepped around the chair and knocked on the door.

"Come in," Alexandra called.

William opened the door and rolled Mason through. He closed the door after they entered, pushing Mason to the middle of the room. The queen sat on a couch opposite him.

William and Riley had been in charge for a long time, both of them given free rein to do what was necessary to return Mason to the kingdom. Now, though, Mason was back and in charge.

William moved to the corner of the room, placing his hands at his sides as he looked on.

"Thank you for coming, Mason," the queen said.

"Again, we're grateful you've given us refuge," Mason answered.

The queen nodded. She had shown great respect to Mason's entourage, most likely because she knew how Riley felt about them all.

"We've been studying your Right Hand carefully. You know how important she is to us, as she is to you."

Mason nodded in silent agreement.

The queen continued, "Her wounds are not physical, at least not in the same way yours are. The mage hurt your body, but we think he did more to her. We think he hurt her…" the queen's voice trailed off. "I don't know the word. I've thought about it quite a bit, but I can't figure out how he did it."

She stared at Mason for a second, then said, "You might think I'm crazy, but his wounds are *inside* her. Her mind. Maybe her very soul, if such a thing exists."

"I don't think you're crazy," Mason responded, "but that doesn't do anything to help me fix her. That's all I care about—getting her healthy."

The queen nodded. "Me too. I'm saying soul and mind, but that's because I lack the knowledge to diagnose her."

"Who has the knowledge, then?"

"Well," the queen answered, "the dark mage does, clearly. Other than that, I can only think of one person." She looked away almost wistfully.

"Who?" Mason asked.

"Her name was Linda. I don't even know if she's alive anymore. I actually doubt it. She'd be… Well, as old as this mage of yours, if not older."

"Who is she?"

The queen stood and walked behind the couch. She remained with her back to Mason. "She's the one who started magic here. She's the one who taught the originals. She might even have taught that dark mage. If anyone knows what's happening to Riley, it'll be her—if she's alive."

"Where would she be?" Mason asked, his voice edged.

"It's hard to say," Alexandra murmured. "The last time anyone saw her, she was leaving the continent."

"Why?"

Alexandra turned around, a slight smile on her face. "How old do you think I am?"

"I...I'm sorry. I just thought you might know," Mason answered.

Alexandra's smile widened. "Don't worry about it. I'm not sure why she was leaving, but legend has it that she was heading to the reef. If there are any clues to finding her, that's where we should start."

"And you think this Linda can save Riley? You think she'll know what's going on with her?" Mason asked.

"I think that if anyone knows, it'll be her. The Chosen are extremely adept at magic, but I can't touch what is going on with her. None of my people can either." Alexandra's face grew grave. "As much as you want to save Riley, understand I want it at least as much. She is our Savior, whether you believe it or not. She will change mankind. It's important that we go west again."

William felt the need to speak up then, although he didn't want to. This was a meeting between leaders, but William had a duty to New Perth, even before his duty to Riley.

"I apologize, sir, but I feel I must say something." He stepped away from the wall. "What about New Perth?

What if Rendal survived? He will surely still be coming for our kingdom."

Mason didn't turn around to look at William, only nodded his head. "You're right. We cannot forget our obligation, and I appreciate you reminding me." He focused again on the queen. "I'm going to head back to New Perth. I have to warn my father and help prepare the kingdom. William will go with you and your Chosen to find this woman, Linda."

The queen nodded in agreement. "We'll have to bring her with us. Whatever is happening, it's getting worse, not better. If we find Linda, we won't have time to return here. It'll be too late."

Mason turned his chair around and looked at William. "You keep her safe, you understand? Not just because we love her, but because she's the only fucking person who can stop Rendal."

"Yes, sir. I'll give my life for her." William was solemn in his promise.

"All right," the queen interjected. "Let's go find this woman and get Riley healed. I'm ready to see her kick some serious fucking ass."

FINIS

AUTHOR NOTES - JACE MITCHELL

DECEMBER 20, 2018

That was intense!

I honestly had no idea how this book was going to end. I could see Riley winding her way to Rendal, learning more and more about her powers, but I didn't understand what would happen when they met. Was she strong enough yet?

Turns out, no. But to me, that feels a lot like real life. How many times do we have to try something over and over again before we're finally able to master it, or to move past some obstacle? The thing I love about Riley is that as long as there is breath in her lungs, she's going to keep trying. Rendal will have to kill her to make her stop hunting him.

Full disclosure, I haven't started Book 4 yet, so I'm not sure what's going to happen. We know the mythology of Arcadia and how the Founder spread the use of magic there, but we don't yet know how it happened in Australia. I'm really, really excited to explore the mythology and how New Perth and Sidnie came to be.

It looks like things are grim for Riley; I've said this

before, but I don't really know what is going to happen to characters. They lead me and I just describe what I see. I do believe, however, that Riley's going to rise. There's a lot of fight left in her, and while she may be down, she's not nearly out.

Okay, back to the salt mines for me. I hope you're ready for book 4!

All the best,
Jace

AUTHOR NOTES - MICHAEL ANDERLE

DECEMBER 25, 2018

THANK YOU for not only reading this story but these *Author Notes* as well.

(I think I've been good with always opening with "thank you." If not, I need to edit the other *Author Notes*!)

RANDOM (*sometimes*) THOUGHTS?

You know, I suggest that if a certain author (*cough* *JACE* *cough*) keeps making my poor Riley get in these situations, I'm going to have to put their email address (or at least a forward email address) in these author notes so the fans can have a few words with them.

And I will ratchet it up from there.

If Jace didn't live so far away from me, I could be a little more personal in my application of subjective collaboration disagreement force.

But, alas, I cannot (and I am *FAR* too lazy to actually get on a plane to do anything.)

Although, the story comes through here (digitally) for editing…

HOW TO MARKET FOR BOOKS YOU LOVE

We are able to support our efforts with you reading our books, and we appreciate you doing this!

If you enjoyed this or ANY book by any author, especially Indie-published, we always appreciate if you make the time to review a book, since it lets other readers who might be on the fence to take a chance on it as well.

AROUND THE WORLD IN 80 DAYS

One of the interesting (at least to me) aspects of my life is the ability to work from anywhere and at any time. In the future, I hope to re-read my own *Author Notes* and remember my life as a diary entry.

Merry Christmas, 2018!

We are in our La Puente (California) home for the first time on Christmas. This also means that we have (had) NO Christmas decorations.

After many years of having a much larger home (with a LOT of storage space, and this house is neither that large, nor does it have much storage space) I am trying to keep our decorations down.

BUT, I still was sulking because we had NONE here. (I'm an author, so I'm allowed to sulk. It helps the empathy of my stories come out. You know, I have to feel them, right?)

Hey, that's my story, and I'm sticking to it!

So, back to the Christmas stuff. We purchased two big

red wreaths (front door and what turned out to be for the mailbox), two boxes of lights (they went around the fireplace) and six little tree decorations (three little angels, and three little stockings that say 'JOY' with a green wreath about 3" around. No, seriously, these are tiny little things.)

It took about ten minutes to put everything up, and it is JUST enough holiday's for me to feel good about having the holiday.

Now I need cookies... (See you later, I'm starving!)

FAN PRICING

If you would like to find out what LMBPN is doing and the books we will be publishing, just sign up at http://lmbpn.com/email/. When you sign up, we notify you of books coming out for the week, any new posts of interest in the books and pop culture arena, and the fan pricing on Saturday.

Ad Aeternitatem,

Michael Anderle

Knight's Creed (1) – Knight's Struggle (2) – Knight's Justice (3) - Etheric Knight (4)

THE HIDDEN MAGIC CHRONICLES

with Justin Sloan

Shades of Light (1) – Shades of Dark (2) – Shades of Glory (3) – Shades of Justice (4)

PATH OF HEROES

with Brandon Barr

Rogue Mage (1)

HAND OF JUSTICE

with Jace Mitchell

The Dark Mage (1) - Chasing Madness (2) - Magic Rising (3)